Praise for Decimated Dreams

"*Decimated Dreams* by Brennan LaFaro is the utterly beguiling and harrowing sequel to *Slattery Falls*. Creepy. Heartfelt. Panic inducing. This book showcases a writer who knows how to turn the screw of horror and unsettle his readers, forcing them to turn the pages and discover how this nightmare ends."

— Ross Jeffery, Bram Stoker Award-Nominated author of *Tome*

"*Decimated Dreams* plunges the reader deep into the writhing center of *Slattery Falls* with little warning and no remorse, building on a growing unease until the unimaginable takes shape. With a deft hand, LaFaro rides the line between despair and hope, all the while asking, "What would you do for family?"

— Anthony J. Rapino,
author of *Tommy of the Order of Cosmic Champions*

"LaFaro's sequel to the excellent *Slattery Falls* comes out swinging with a wicked twist on the missing child storyline. Told from Elsie's darkly humorous perspective, she and Travis must once again enter the evil clutches of the small town that almost killed them, this time in an attempt to save their precious, young daughter. LaFaro doesn't hold back on the constant dread and twists, and the final line will have readers rabid for more."

— Heather Levy, Anthony Award-Nominated author of *Walking Through Needles*

"LaFaro writes with the class of Charles Dickens, the ingenuity of Sir Arthur Conan Doyle, and the zest of Stephen King. *Decimated Dreams* spotlights LaFaro's ability to cultivate a familiar story, only it's in a way and place you can't begin to navigate as anything but the spectator.

This one had me in a throat grip for nearly the whole trip. To lose a child can be such a fine path to walk, but LaFaro exudes paranoia, near-hopelessness, and the utmost determination to drop every single thing in the world to find your baby.

If that ending doesn't compel you to beg for the next installment, someone should check your pulse… Slattery Falls may have claimed another soul."

— Patrick R. McDonough, editor of *Hot Iron and Cold Blood: An Anthology of the Weird West*

ISBN 978-1-63789-729-4

For information address Crossroad Press at 141 Brayden Dr., Hertford, NC 27944

A Macabre Ink Production - Macabre Ink is an imprint of Crossroad Press.

www.crossroadpress.com

First edition

For Rachel,
Watch the woods for
green-eyed weirdos.

DECIMATED DREAMS

SLATTERY FALLS BOOK TWO

BRENNAN LAFARO

04.07.23

Macabre Ink

For Aron,
Whose cool gunpowder glare still lays me bare.

The Story So Far...

Drawn together by an affinity for exploring haunted houses, Travis, Elsie, and Josh soon discover that something is hunting them. Robert Weeks, an undead menace with penetrating sea-green eyes, seeks to collect all three in an effort to sustain his immortality. Following a brush with Weeks, the trio decides to give paranormal investigations a rest.

After ten years of silence, Elsie and Travis are married and living normal, if unexciting, lives, but Josh still dwells in the past. Josh discovers a link between Robert Weeks and a string of missing children's cases spanning back more than a century. He tracks Weeks to a house in Slattery Falls, Massachusetts, using the diary of Emily Stone, a woman who witnessed Weeks' rise to power in the late nineteenth century. The three travel to Slattery Falls and navigate the labyrinthian basement of the Weeks House to summon Tabitha, Weeks' deceased wife, in order to put a stop to his reign of terror.

In a last-ditch effort to stop the summoning ritual, Weeks kills Josh, tearing his arm from his body and delivering a fatal blow to the head, but Josh's sacrifice is not in vain. Tabitha appears in a flash of white light and ferries Robert Weeks away. The moment he disappears, the house begins to shake. It collapses into a heap of rubble only seconds after Travis and Elsie escape.

Travis and Elsie return home to try and pick up the pieces of their lives, hoping that they've truly put a stop to the disappearances and made the world safer, especially once they discover they have a child of their own on the way.

PART ONE

Every Thought A Thought of You

CHAPTER ONE

"ELSIE!" Travis' scream echoed through the underground grotto. It bounced off the low cavernous ceiling, clambered down the stone walls, and shot across the shoulder-deep water, which suddenly felt very cold.

A glow from beneath the water provided a flawless view of Travis' face. Fear consumed every feature. His eyelids drew back, giving way to the whites of his eyes, and his jaw hung so low I worried he might sample the water.

He reached toward me, half running and half swimming through the murky pool. From the corner of my eye, I saw Josh stumble as he followed, then regain his balance. His brow furrowed. He had no idea what was wrong with my husband either.

Within a few feet of me, Travis came to a sloshing stop. His face cleared at the same time.

"What? Travis, what's wrong?" I asked, matching the concern in his eyes from a moment ago.

He pivoted his head around, studying every inch of the grotto except my eyes. "Nothing. I thought I saw something, but the light… must be playing tricks on me."

I tried to track his line of sight, but whatever he'd seen remained locked away within him. "You're scaring me. You sure you're alright?"

"Yeah, let's just get out of here."

Robert Weeks' basement had fucked with my mind—hell, all of our minds—enough for one day, and I could do without any more hallucinations or disappearing walls.

I continued forward, keeping an eye on Travis and watching for dangers at the same time. Josh and Travis wandered away to resume their exploration. Their lowered voices carried across the grotto, maneuvering around the underground cavern's strange acoustics. Travis held up his end of the mumbled conversation but glanced over his shoulder at me every few steps. The distance garbled their words, but it appeared they'd discovered something. I turned to join them and my shoulder scraped against something solid and rough.

A wall.

How had I missed that?

I pressed both palms against the coarse surface just above the water line. No give. Not an illusion, then. The throbbing in my shoulder confirmed this. A warm wetness that had nothing to do with water trickled down my arm. My feet should have met some resistance, but nothing blocked their path. I swung a foot forward and hit only water. Swishing it around, my foot collided with what felt like the sides of an underwater tunnel.

I yanked my leg free and returned it to solid ground, then called for the boys.

"What are we looking at?" said Travis, squinting at the patch of wall in front of me.

"There's a hole in the wall, under the surface." I drew his attention to the surface of the water right above the opening. "Feel here."

He copied my stance, pressing his hands against the wall and kicking around with his leg. "How does that help us?" Travis asked.

I'm not sure he caught my eye-roll, but it was there.

"We've come this far," said Josh. "We swim through it. The path continues on the other side." Always the problem-solver, never the volunteer.

The suggestion hung in the stagnant air for only a moment, but I knew it had to be me. We didn't know how long the tunnel would continue and I'd seen Travis get winded walking to the mailbox.

"I'll do it," I volunteered. "Scope it out."

He argued. Predictably. Don't get me wrong, I loved the white knight mantle he'd adopted since we arrived, but it was old three obstacles ago.

"You finished?"

No reply to that. Just those godawful puppy dog eyes. I swear I almost caved and sent him, but then he would've kept pulling out chairs and opening car doors until I eventually had to kill him.

"Thirty seconds, tops."

Travis grabbed my face, placing his fingertips just beneath my ears. They were cold and pruny, but still comforting. His eyes lost their sympathetic edge, narrowing into a firm strength. The message came through loud and clear. Pleading became acceptance. "There's no way I can talk you out of this, is there?"

"Not a one." I disappeared beneath the water before he could say another word and wriggled through the opening, tinged with a light-green hue, no doubt a result of the lights emanating from the bottom of the pool. I wouldn't call myself skinny, and the squeeze agreed, but it allowed me passage. A sharp wave of panic struck as my feet followed me through the entrance. Would I have enough room to turn around if it was a dead end?

The thought died quickly as I drifted into a connected pool of clear blue water. Compared to the murkiness that hid our feet in the grotto, it appeared almost tropical. A passing neon clownfish would have fit right in. I'd been under for less than fifteen seconds, at a guess, but I sucked in a breath of air when I surfaced. A haze of green light surrounded the base of the tunnel. At least I'd be able to find my way back easy enough. The water on this side appeared cleaner, but the air didn't taste any fresher.

I froze, tracking movement in my peripheral vision, but when I turned there was nothing there. After rubbing the water from my eyes, I kept as still as possible to draw out whatever lay in wait. I caught it again, but it wasn't movement exactly. The edges of the cavern blurred when I looked away from them, like a child's chalk drawing. As soon as I focused on the hazy patch of wall, it returned to high definition.

A few feet of water separated me from the stony path which dipped down into the grotto like a boat ramp. The rest of the underground chasm was small and unremarkable. As my face dried, the edges of my vision continued to appear out of focus. The sensation made my stomach feel uneasy, suspended in an extended form of roller-coaster-drop. After a brief inspection, the walls offered no other exits. I turned my head back toward the boat ramp and my heart jumped into my throat at the sight of a dark figure standing there.

The water turned arctic cold. It crept over every inch of my skin. It wasn't Weeks. I'd only seen him in bits and pieces so far, but this figure didn't possess the broad shoulders and towering stature. Lanky with greasy, stringy hair hanging in its face, this person resembled a gaunt creature more than a human being. A trench coat wrapped its angular frame, closed at the center and covering God-only-knew what. Besides the face, which leered from behind the curtains of hair with terrible glowing green eyes, the only patches of skin evident were its feet, filthy and bare with the jagged overgrown toenails of an animal. It cocked its head, openly curious about the person treading water in its lair.

He waits.

A voice cut through the silence, groaning like rusty gears powering a run-down machine.

My feet kicked to keep me afloat. I wanted to dive back below the water and return to Travis, to Josh, but the only actions my body allowed were the most basic ones to keep me from drowning.

At the bottom of the stairs. He waits.

The same voice. Its mouth didn't show through the mangy hair, but

I was sure it didn't move. The sound came from inside my head, rattling around like a migraine.

I fought a desire to cover my ears, knowing it wouldn't help, but desperate to rid my brain of that invasive sound. The figure stepped to the side—no, that's not quite right. It slid to the side, like gravity relocating an oil slick. It extended a bony claw to reveal a tunnel previously blocked. Despite every signal in my body telling me to dive back down and flee, I moved closer.

My feet struggled for purchase on the slippery slant rising out of the water and I stepped forward, drawn like a moth to flame. Adrenaline lowered my inhibitions, but I retained enough self-control to stop well short of the figure and see where he pointed. Another flight of stairs loomed behind him. The same stairs we'd avoided just before entering the grotto. Don't ask how I know, I just do.

But that's not where he pointed. I followed the single grimy, outstretched finger with my eyes to the entrance I'd come through. The surface still glowed a faint green that matched the figure's eyes.

A shiver ran through my body and the voice returned, drilling into my head.

He waits.

The same blathering bullshit over again.

At the bottom of the stairs. He waits.

Heard it all before.

Tonight, he falls.

This was new.

The creature turned its head toward me, as if to ensure it had my attention. It did. Moisture dripped down my body—a mixture of the viscous water splashing around my knees and a nervous sweat. A cold sweat. The worst kind.

Three will descend. Two will escape.

"What?" I said out loud, and immediately felt stupid. This thing didn't communicate with me. It communicated *at* me. Black strings of hair fluttered in the dormant air of the cavern. Its eyes stared at me from behind the locks.

He waits. He waits. He waits. He waits. He waits.

An endless loop, the same intonation accompanied every utterance of the two syllables.

Three will descend. Two will escape.

"No!" I screamed. "You don't get to decide that!"

He waits. He waits. He waits. He waits. He waits.

Laughter joined the chanting, creating a crazed harmony while the creature remained perfectly still, with a second track playing over the repeated mantra. The high-pitched barking grated my nerves. My teeth clenched in a fruitless attempt to shut it out. I tried to scream again but it wouldn't come. The underground cave spun and the water rose, climbing my legs to envelop the top half of my body with icy liquid. I slammed my eyes shut and sucked in a deep breath as the pool pulled me under like a riptide.

I barely had time to lament the loss of control before my face broke the surface. I hyperventilated, not needing the air but gasping in panicked breaths all the same. My gaze shot toward the top of the ramp, but the creature wasn't there. The voice and the laughter were gone.

Gone.

The word echoed through my head. I'd been over here far too long. I couldn't believe Travis hadn't already barreled through the goddamn wall like the Kool-Aid Man. Sucking in one more deep breath, I dove back through the underwater tunnel, nearly colliding with someone trying to enter from the other side.

Travis.

Clasped together, we breached the surface. He spoke but I couldn't make out the words. I felt his lips on mine and the dizziness drained away. The chill deep within my core began to thaw. I hated this place, but for a moment I was home in his arms. The cavern's echoes caught up with me all at once.

"It's not far," I said, wiping water from my face and paying attention to the corners of my vision. No blur, no haze. My feet touched solid ground beneath the water. I hadn't realized how much I missed that while floating on the other side of the wall. "It comes up into another room with only about ten feet of water, then it leads back up onto the floor like a boat ramp."

The figure, my mind screamed. *The warnings. I'd been gone for so long. Why weren't they more worried?*

Panic swam—maybe not the best choice of words, but certainly the closest to the front of my mind—through my brain. We'd seen a giant of a man appear from thin air then disappear earlier that day. We'd seen the ghosts of the children stolen and murdered by Robert Weeks. We'd seen the house bend space and time to reshape itself to his will. *We* remained the one constant in all those experiences.

I'd seen the nightmare creature. Me alone. It spoke inside my head.

Throughout every wild experience I'd shared with Travis and Josh, we looked to each other first. Gauge the reactions of the other two before proclaiming something paranormal or supremely fucked up.

This experience belonged to me alone, and that meant one of two things. One, I hallucinated the entire thing, staying underwater until my brain nearly popped. That combined with the stress this place had me under could do it. If that was the case, I couldn't let Travis know the cave had gotten to me. Broken me.

Two, Weeks sent me that vision alone for a reason. Until I could figure out what that reason might be, I needed to keep it to myself. To not allow him the upper hand. Guilt radiated through my entire body, an embarrassed heat that temporarily kept the cold at bay. I desperately needed a compelling reason to keep this from Travis. Not being the only one keeping a secret provided little solace.

I half-smiled and continued. "You won't love what's on the other side, though."

"Oh shit. It's fucking stairs again, isn't it?" Disappointment crept into Travis' tone, but the worry had picked up and left for the moment. I'd done a competent job of hiding the dread instilled in me by the creature's manic prophecies. Hiding them from Travis, anyway. Josh's narrowed eyes told me that liar recognized liar.

Three will descend. Two will escape.

A lump formed in my throat. How could I live without one of them?

"Stairs," I confirmed with a nod. With nothing left to say, we dove one by one and disappeared into the underwater tunnel. Oddly enough, the light reflecting off the tunnel no longer shined green, but displayed the disappointingly dull gray of poured concrete.

CHAPTER TWO

Five Years Later

"Mommy!"

A cannonball struck me square in the gut, smashing what remained of my sleep to smithereens and banishing the remnants of the dream. At least for one more night. This particular cannonball was blessed with a big toothy grin and beautiful blue eyes. Her name was April.

Travis never admitted to wishing for a boy—maybe he never consciously did—but oh how his eyes lit up when we talked about names. If it were a boy, we would call him Josh—never Joshua. No room for debate there after Uncle Josh's sacrifice. Impatient as we were, when the eighteen-week mark rolled around and the doctor asked if we'd like to know the sex, Travis and I both said "yes" at the same time, nearly tripping over each other. The air practically buzzed as we waited for the news.

Dr. Campbell, a kindly old man who successfully guided two green-around-the-gills newbies through nine months of the process, peered over the top of his glasses and told us it was a girl.

"How positive?" asked Travis. A hint of disappointment in his voice quickly vanished under the weight of a euphoric smile. Tears gathered at the corner of his eyes, and I'll never forget how much I loved him just then.

Dr. Campbell looked pleased. Wrinkles formed around his eyes as he smiled. "Mr. Morland, I've been doing this for quite some time. I won't pretend I've never made a mistake, but it gets rarer and rarer with age. I'm quite certain you and Mrs. Morland will be welcoming a lovely little girl in twenty weeks or so."

Travis nodded. I'd seen the vacant look on his face plenty of times. It meant hundreds of responses were flying through his brain, but the right one eluded him. The best decision in those instances always proved to be silent agreement.

We brainstormed girls names that night. Set on Josh for so long, neither of us wanted to consider that it wouldn't work out. Eager to honor my cousin's memory, I tossed out Tabitha, but a dark cloud crossed Travis' face, and I wished I could snatch the suggestion back. Not anger, but fear.

"I don't know," he said. The cloud dissipated as he scratched the back of his neck, then began fiddling with his wedding ring. "Just feels like a bad omen, Els."

His eyes glazed over in a flash, and then just as quickly, he snapped out of it.

"You alright there? I could almost smell the light bulb's burning filaments." I swirled my finger around the top of my head.

"Filaments?"

"Not important. What are you thinking about?"

"April."

"The month?"

He closed his eyes and shook his head. "No, that's her name. Do you love it?"

I did, actually. Despite the fact I was almost positive he'd named our daughter after a Ninja Turtles character, that was her name. A little-known fact you can't understand until it happens to you—when you hear your child's name for the first time, it shines like a beacon, and you wonder how you survived so long without its vital light.

"Her name is April."

After April splashed into our bed, I rubbed the sleep from my eyes and wrapped her in a combination of hugs and blanket.

Cannonball.

Splash.

All these thoughts of water; the dream came roaring back.

Travis turned over, his eyes still plastered shut. April had weaseled her way up to the top of the bed after flattening me like a pancake. He laid an arm over her and forced his eyes open to meet mine.

"You had that dream again." No question. No patronizing tone. We both had the emotional scars to prove that day happened, and we'd never take a resurfacing memory of it lightly.

I forced a smile, but didn't deny it.

His mind had filled some of the blanks in the dream and I let it happen. He knew I dreamt of the figure in the grotto. One of the workers, he called it. We saw the same creatures trying to escape the collapsing house later on, and evidently he and Josh had seen one a long time ago. Before I entered the equation.

I understood he wasn't brushing me off when he told me that dream never happened. His rationale came down to timing. When I first described the dream in detail, he focused on every word, his eyes locked on mine with a worried expression. When I finished, he drew me into a smothering hug.

"The way you describe it," he said. "There's no way it all occurred in half a minute."

I agreed. How could I not?

"You were gone for thirty seconds. Maybe less. I counted. Probably too fast," he chuckled, "and when I hit thirty, I dove in and found you."

He was right. Half a minute was barely enough time to swim through, poke my head up and look around, then come back. But it happened. The few times it came up—did it happen or not—I did something I swore I never would. I lied to him. Told him I was being silly, and of course, it couldn't have happened that way.

Except I think he was trying to convince himself more than me.

Travis held my gaze a moment, judging the authenticity of the smile. Satisfied, he turned his attention to April and blew raspberries on her stomach until he drew out the belly laugh we loved so much. Perhaps because it's a sound that can't be faked.

With April still delirious from tickle-related laughter, Travis picked up a remote from his nightstand and clicked on the stereo. The muted guitar and subdued vocals of My Chemical Romance's "Helena" poured from the speakers.

I raised an eyebrow at Travis and he shrugged. "Helps me wake up." He lowered the volume before the drums could kick in.

"What are you doing up so early, squirt?" I asked, once April settled down. "The sun's barely awake. The birds have to wipe the sleep from their eyes before they can sing their song."

"I couldn't sleep," she said. "I woke up before the sun, and I tried to go back to sleep like you said. I even shut my eyes as tight as I could, but I can't sleep."

I stuck my bottom lip out at her. "Oh, baby, what got you up in the first place?"

"The man." She looked away, kneading the sheets on our bed. "The one who stands at my window."

The hair on my arms stood straight up and an icy chill slithered down my spine. April continued to fidget with the sheets as Travis and I looked at each other over the top of her head. The color drained from his face and his eyes widened. We were back in the grotto again. I swear I could almost see the lights dancing on the walls.

Leaving April tucked into our bed, we raced for her room.

The music played for her alone.

CHAPTER THREE

Red and blue waves of light threw strange shapes and patterns across the exterior of our small Southbridge residence, making it resemble the inside of a lava lamp. Travis, April, and I huddled on the sidewalk near an idling cruiser while neighbors gawked out their windows and a half-dozen uniformed officers searched the house, inside and out.

It had been fifteen years since the research into the Benson House, yet every detail about the case remained fresh in my head. The parallels were too eerie to ignore.

In that case, the officers found nothing. In ours, it was close enough to result in indifference. They sympathized with our plight and didn't appear to be skimping on the job. There just wasn't anything else to find. No forced entry to the house. No evidence anyone had been near April's window, except a little doll made of straw and bound with red twine, tucked next to a daylily. A little creepy, but perfectly innocuous except for our inability to explain what it was or how it got there. It fit comfortably into a small evidence bag and the police took it away.

We stood on the front lawn, shivering in the October morning air while the other officers performed one more cursory search. The neighborhood was deserted except for a single commuter who slowed to gawk on the way to his car. When I met his eyes he moved faster, as if recalling an important appointment. I tried to think of his name but drew a blank. We had moved into the house almost ten years earlier and could barely pick our neighbors out of a lineup.

Travis slid his wedding ring off his fourth finger, flipped the black tungsten carbide band over, and replaced it. I watched him perform the nervous maneuver over and over. Before I could snap at him to stop, a female officer a few years older than Travis and me approached. Officer Metcalf had shoulder-length brown hair and a face that seemed too soft for law enforcement, too kind. She hunkered down in a crouch next to April. A warm smile lit up her face, cutting through the dour morning and putting me at ease. Judging by the way April relinquished her death grip on my hand, she felt alright with the woman, as well.

"Hey, honey," said Officer Metcalf. "Sorry we had to drag you out here in your PJs. You warm enough?"

"Mmhmm," April mumbled, not meeting the woman's eyes just yet.

"I know you've had a rough morning, kid, but would you mind if we talked about it? If it's okay with your parents, that is."

The officer's eyes darted up, looking to us for permission. Travis and I nodded in sync. Two puppets sharing the same string.

Metcalf returned her eyes to April, but kept quiet until the little girl answered.

"Okay," whispered April, so soft that a windier morning might have carried it away.

"Thank you, hon. I appreciate that." She motioned toward the curb next to the police car with her head. "Can we go sit down? If I keep crouching like this, I'm going to get stuck. Then I'll have to spend the rest of the day walking like a crab." She scuttled side to side, making April burst into a fit of giggles. I may have allowed a smile to sneak onto my face, as well.

"That would be nice," said April, surprising me. "Can Mom and Dad come? Only I'm not supposed to go with strangers."

"Of course," said Metcalf, leading April to the curb and plopping down with a sigh. "I bet Mom and Dad taught you that. Very wise. I hope you know you can talk to me though, and if I ask a question you don't like, or you don't want to talk to me anymore, you can run off back to Mom and Dad." She leaned in, lowering her voice, but not so soft I couldn't hear. "I won't even be offended."

"What's offended?"

"Offended is when you get upset because someone did something you didn't like."

"Okay. I'll try not to offend you, police lady."

Metcalf laughed, even adding a knee slap for effect. "How about this, April? How about you call me Robin, like the bird. Just promise you won't tell any of the men around here. They all have to call me Officer Metcalf, but *you* have special permission."

April mimicked the laugh and even slapped her own knee. "Okay. Robin." The sound of the woman's name drew a smile across April's lovely face.

Robin let April have the moment of levity, then gradually allowed the smile to slip from her face. "April, your parents told me you saw a man outside your window. Is that right?"

Any progress the officer had made with the five-year-old soared out the window like a... well, like a robin. April clammed up and studied her toes, wiggling free from the ends of her sandals.

"We didn't have time to find her shoes," I said, feeling my cheeks grow hot.

Robin continued. "I know you probably don't want to talk about it much, April, and that's okay, but it's also not okay for anyone to make you feel unsafe. If someone is making you feel that way, it's my job to make sure they can't do that anymore."

April's tough exterior started to crack. Any minute now, she would sing like a… Shit. A canary. I held my breath, nerves creeping through my body. Not because I didn't want her to share, but because I feared what might come out of her mouth. How could I possibly hold back a scream if she told the officer the man outside her window stood taller than a giant with a massive red beard, like fire enveloping his face?

Travis and I always took care not to mention anything about that day when small ears might be listening. It's possible she heard us while faking sleep one night, but the alternative scared me considerably more. Someday she'd ask how Dad and I met. We'd give her a carefully curated version of the story and take her to visit Uncle Josh's empty grave, but that day waited far in the future.

"So what do you think?" Robin's voice snapped me back to reality. "Can you help me do my job? Keep you safe?"

"I never saw him," said April, her eyes not leaving her feet. "Not all the way. I looked at the window and it was… smoky outside."

"Smoky?" murmured Robin.

"Like foggy, sweetie?" asked Travis, clearly forgetting we were invisible. A subtle kick to the shin reminded him.

April shrugged.

"April, honey." Robin paused, searching for the right words. "I need you to know I believe you before I ask my next question. Do you believe that?"

"Yes."

"Good. That's good. If it was foggy outside your window, how do you know someone was out there?"

"I saw his eyes. Even with the smoke. They were green. Kind of like the grass, but not the same."

"Like the ocean," I whispered.

My heart stopped beating for a second, then started again. Hard. From the corner of my eye, I saw Travis faring no better. The officer asked a few more questions, but the sound of her voice resembled static, a television turned up to top volume stuck between channels.

CHAPTER FOUR

"He's back," said Travis, as he paced frantically up and down the hall. April sat in front of PBS Kids with some Goldfish crackers after the police left, awash in its safe glow, while we attempted a civil discussion about what to do next. Somehow the police's suggestions, such as setting the alarm system during the day and having April sleep in our bed for a few nights, rang a little hollow.

"He's back, he's back, he's back, what the fuck, he's back."

The civil discussion lacked civility.

"Think about it, Trav. How could he be back? We watched him get yanked to another fucking plane of existence."

"We don't know what we saw! This ghost shit, undead shit, it's way above our clearance level. Josh would know…"

A single slip in tense and my mind transported me to Weeks' basement. Feet trapped in concrete and helpless to do anything while Weeks mangled Josh and then beat him to death in front of our eyes. Five years on, and I swear we still forgot Josh was gone sometimes.

Three will descend. Two will escape.

My fault.

"You're right," I whispered. An attempt to bring inside voices back to the conversation. "Josh would've known exactly what to do, and if he didn't, he would've sat his ass in front of Google until he did. But he's not here, because he gave his life for you. For me. And April."

"He didn't know April."

"That doesn't mean he didn't have her in mind when Weeks cracked his head open."

Travis winced. It replaced the hardened, somewhat manic look on his face as he paraded up and down the hall in his bathrobe, then melted to worry. Fear. Not "I just saw a ghost" fear, but the kind a parent feels when they first understand that the world is too big and scary to protect their children from everything it holds.

"I don't know what to do," he said, putting words to what his face had already told me.

"Me either, but we'll figure it out." I faked a smile. Travis matched it, but his eyes told me he knew it was for show. "In the meantime, we won't leave her alone and give him the chance to pull a Benson. With any luck, it's all a false alarm." I paused for a moment, trying to decide if I really wanted to ask the next question.

"Is there anything out of the ordinary that's happened lately?"

Travis didn't rush a "no" out at me. His head rolled back and he thought about it before he said it.

"Doesn't matter how small or insignificant, anything at all."

He shook his head. I wish I could say I believed him, but he had a history of trying to protect me from perceived danger. "You?"

"The dream, but that's nothing new. Never went away really."

"Green eyes, Els," he said, changing the subject so abruptly that it left skid marks. His mind was all over the place. Mine was, too. "That's such a specific goddamn detail."

"So what do we do? The police aren't going to act on anything. That one officer was nice, but even she probably thinks we're overreacting to a five-year-old's imagination."

"She sleeps in our bed, for starters. And then... Christ, I don't know. We can't..." Tears formed at the corner of his eyes, accompanying a fear I hoped I'd never have to see again. An audible gulp made room for the rest of the sentence. "We can't watch her every minute. He knows that, counts on it."

"We have to try."

The accounts we had gathered from a variety of sources about the disappearances in Slattery Falls more than confirmed this. Kids disappeared in the literal blink of an eye. If Weeks had returned, he might not even need us to blink. Over the course of centuries, maybe millennia, he'd learned how to manipulate reality. I had no more words to offer comfort so I hoped my eyes said what I couldn't as I squeezed Travis' hand. He didn't squeeze back.

"We could go away," he whispered.

"What?"

"We know his reach extends at least to Southwestern Connecticut. We always assumed it went at least that far in every other direction. So we leave that circle. Go to Tennessee, New Mexico, Seattle, California. Who cares? Just get the fuck out of Dodge."

"And not come back?"

"I don't know. Maybe." His eyes pleaded with me to overlook the impulsiveness, the fear, and see the reason hidden within. And I could. Sort of. I believed April and I feared the worst. But wasn't there the slightest chance the police were right? That we were caving to the imagination of a kid who had it in spades?

Careful, like tiptoeing between fault lines, I answered, running my thumb along his knuckles as I did. "We can't just beg off work, can't just abandon the house, the bills."

If possible, his eyes went wider. I shook my head. He tried to pull his hand away, but I wouldn't let him. "I'm not saying we can't go, that it's a bad idea, but… Tomorrow, okay?"

"Tomorrow," he repeated, as if I'd spoken the word in an unfamiliar language.

"Tomorrow afternoon. Enough time for both of us to try and set something up with work. Put it in as vacation or take unpaid time off. Whatever we need to do to make sure we're not broke and unemployed if it's a false flag."

I caught him as his mouth opened to argue. "I'll call out of work tomorrow, see what I can sort out over the phone. You go in, make sure we can afford that lavish vacation. I'll keep April tethered to me all day. We'll pack light and hop in the car the moment Dad gets home from work. No fucking around."

He searched for the right words to move the timeline up, but couldn't find them.

"She'll sleep with us tonight, as much sleep as we can manage anyway. Maybe even camp out here," I said, intent on pushing my luck.

He blinked, then let out a sigh. "Okay."

The search and interviews had taken most of the day, which left Travis and me just enough time to prepare a half-assed dinner and putter around with one eye on April at all times. I imagined the worst with every step. The room might fill with mist, leaving only two glowing green fog lights in the haze. The walls of our home could change on a whim and seal us off from each other. Worst of all, I envisioned April's cold form splayed across the living room floor, skin pale as alabaster, her final breath stolen.

The sun went down and afternoon turned into evening which turned into night. If April thought it strange that we didn't pull her away from the television, she wasn't about to draw attention to it. The living room felt, if not safe, at least comfortable. Dawn was when the man with the green eyes arrived at her window. In the morning, when he peered in, her little bed would be empty.

Autumn in Massachusetts brings with it the occasional Nor'easter, a storm with near hurricane-force winds and copious amounts of rain. These storms usually strike with enough warning to prepare for them, unless you've tuned the television to PBS all day and ignored your phone.

It actually fit in with our plans of huddling in the living room for the night, wrapped in warm blankets and together in case the power went out or a branch crashed through a window. We made a night of it, so long as the power stayed on, watching movies and making popcorn, all in service of keeping a little girl from fear.

With safety at a premium, nobody slept well because the wind howled all night and the trees creaked as powerful gusts strained them where the thinner wood at the base of each branch met the strong trunk. Every creak delivered the expectation that one of the ageless behemoths in the backyard would crash through the roof, bringing nature inside in an unwelcome way.

When April could no longer keep her eyes open, I encouraged Travis to get some rest. One of us had work in the morning and we couldn't hop on a westbound interstate with the driver passed out at the steering wheel. Their soft snores gave me comfort while I paced to keep my eyes from growing heavy.

I don't remember falling asleep.

I don't even remember sitting down.

I walked a patch of carpet from the kitchen to the living room and back, turning my head on a swivel like a ballet dancer, determined not to take my attention off that precious little girl for so much as a second. Haze danced around the light bulbs, the way it does when your eyes want their lids to tuck them in. The plush carpet absorbed the impact of each footstep, a fluffy, almost marshmallow-like substance, inviting me to lay down for just a moment.

That's where I found myself the next morning. Warm sunlight beat against my closed eyelids, but that's not what woke me up. It was Travis, screaming as though an ancient force of evil had torn away one of his limbs. In a way, it had.

April was gone.

CHAPTER FIVE

Reading the stories of the missing children in Slattery Falls tore at my heartstrings. Diving into the history of Todd Benson, especially the detailed struggle his parents went through to find him, nearly reduced me to a whimpering mess.

When it's your child, the experience is different. It's the hope that hurts the most. The average household contains countless places to hide. Most of them wouldn't conceal even the smallest child, but that doesn't stop you from checking them. April had stuffed herself into plenty of impossible places before, only to jump out and surprise us with that big toothy grin. Our couch sits four inches off the floor, yet I lifted the cover to check. My heart soared at the prospect of finding April's smiling face peering out, the winner of a hide-and-seek game I hadn't known we were playing.

Travis and I checked other equally absurd places, and despite what we knew but couldn't bring ourselves to say out loud, our belief that we would find her kept us going. With each hiding place exhausted several times over, Travis stood catching his breath. Not from exertion, but from the type of fear that causes your heart to beat like a marathon runner. I wasn't doing any better.

He chose six simple words, but his tone spoke countless more. There would be no cross-country road trip, not while our family was incomplete.

"We have to call the police."

Not because they can help us, but because that's what people do. They'll put on a show, might even put forth an honest effort, but they won't find her. They'll reassure us that a high percentage of children, so close to one hundred percent it might as well be all, are found in the first few hours. They might even believe their own words.

He was right. We had to call the police.

As expected, the police combed the house and property with unrivaled thoroughness. If a trace of April was there to be found, they would have found it. Their visit from the day before forced them to move with a determined seriousness.

Officer Metcalf delivered all the expected questions and statements, but stopped short of promising they would find April. She implied it, tiptoed around it, but didn't come out and say it. That was probably rule number one in the academy when it came to missing children. The radiant glow that surrounded the officer—Robin, she'd allowed April to call her—didn't make the return journey. A stoic professionalism replaced the warmth that had resided in her face only twenty-four hours earlier. The façade broke only when she handed me a business card.

"That's my personal line. Call it any time," she said, then slipped back among the rest of the blue uniforms.

Hours passed, moving simultaneously too slow and entirely too fast. It resulted in an unsettling mixture of wondering how our baby girl could have disappeared such a short time ago and increasing panic about what might happen if we allowed any more time to pass. The tension between the two emotions made me feel as if I was floating.

Imagine your last memory before slipping into a state of blackout drunk. Your body doesn't belong to you. It stumbles around the house, but without your permission. A voice flows out of your mouth, and it sounds like yours, but you don't remember telling it to speak. You didn't approve the words that dribble out. Your husband takes your hand, squeezes your shoulder, but you're only partially aware. It's happening to someone else.

The police cars keep the red and blue lights off as they pull away. They don't even bother to announce their departure. Instead, their black and white bodies vanish over the horizon and even though you didn't think they could help, you feel more alone than ever once they're out of sight. Your husband speaks gentle and soothing words, but they sound thick and far away. One of you is underwater and it might be you. You can't be sure. Eventually, you're no longer standing. You don't remember going inside, but the couch rises to greet you and it happens so subtly that it comes as a surprise. The cushions are wet and you worry for a second that someone has spilled a drink or maybe the roof is leaking. It's irrational, but isn't all of this? Another second, maybe a minute, passes before you realize the moisture is coming from you, from the same place as that mewling noise. You want to turn it off and rest, but you can't. You try to pull it together, but there's not enough strands to grab hold of. Someone's touching you, a hand on a shoulder, another on your lower back. Probably your husband again trying to bring you back from the void, but you can't be sure. And you don't really care.

The next thing happens quickly. Sleep takes you in such a manner that you didn't even see it coming, wrapping you in its warmth and providing a temporary, yet ultimately false, hope. Your little girl is God-knows-where with God-knows-who, except you do know.

And that's why sleep can't hold you for long.

CHAPTER SIX

My day job granted me a leave of absence, for all it mattered. I wouldn't have gone in anyway. What if she came back while I was out of the house? Travis didn't say it, but I think half the reason he begged off work was to keep an eye on me. Worry twisted his features in every conceivable way. Little red lines, capillaries all too visible in each eyeball, burned with the lack of sleep and his growing amount of concern. Small dark bags took hold under each eye telling the same story. Maybe he didn't think I noticed, but the narrowed eyes and flared nostrils gave him away. He wasn't himself around me, as if what I'd already caused could get any worse from a single misstep.

What *I'd* caused.

I treat Travis like the goof he is, sometimes. A lot. But he's perceptive, and in this case, he had the good sense not to lay down a thick helping of I-told-you-so stew, even though I deserved it.

They—whoever the fuck *they* is—always say you'll never look back from the view on your deathbed and wish you spent more time at the office. It's a weird sentiment because no one needs to think twice before agreeing with it. No shit, of course family is more important than work. And yet, we subconsciously prioritize it on a regular basis. All those small choices group together, adding up in a nearly imperceptible way. We clock in fifteen minutes early. We stay fifteen minutes late. People act appalled at the suggestion they'd pick work over family most of the time because those choices are so rarely set before them in an obvious way, but I'd asked Travis to wait one more day. Nothing subtle about that choice.

The bold girl who didn't used to give two fucks what passersby thought of her fuchsia hair wouldn't have considered job security in a mad dash to avoid a vengeful spirit or save a child. She'd have thrown anything within arms' reach in the back of the car and been outside the confines of New England before lunchtime. Maturity sure as hell has its bondage.

"How long are we going to stay like this?" Travis asked the next afternoon, maybe two days later. Who knew? I slept in fits and time meant exactly shit.

"They'll call." Even with the clarity my fuck-up awarded, a small slice of my brain hoped for a more traditional happy-tears outcome. Maybe April had wandered down the road to our favorite playground. At night she looked up at the same stars as Travis and me, camped underneath the plastic purple slide that always shocked her on the way down. I ninety-nine percent knew it was bullshit, but that last sliver contained enough hope to keep me from going off the deep end.

Because what would we do if *HE* had April?

Travis' silence lasted an uncomfortably long time and the hand that rubbed circles on my lower back paused. "What if they don't? What if there's no trail to go on, nothing to even suggest a kidnapping? There's no phone call that says your kid disappeared into thin air. Poof. Like she never existed."

His words were cruel, but his tone suggested he didn't mean them to be.

"God, Travis. Please, I need you to just say what you mean." I wiped a tear from my eye, knowing if I kept letting them flow, they ran the risk of carving out a gorge, like a river cutting through a canyon over the course of centuries.

"We don't have any way of knowing where he took her, but we know where to start."

"Jesus Christ, I hope you're not suggesting what I think you are."

He continued on like I hadn't said a word. "The house collapsed, probably hasn't been touched since. The town would want to forget it was even there, but what if there's some clue among the ruins? We saw Weeks pass through the doorway to the other side, wherever that is. We put a cap on the whole situation because it was just more goddamn comfortable that way."

"But doors open from both sides."

A glimmer of a smile twitched on his lips, the first sign I'd seen since April went missing. "Did you just quote *The Avengers*?"

"Shut up. You might be on to something. Even Josh..." I gritted my teeth and pretended not to notice Travis tense up at the mention of his best friend. My cousin. "Even he didn't know exactly what he was doing when he summoned Tabitha. At least that's what I got from his letter. Agreed?"

"Agree," he said hesitantly, then waited for me to continue.

"Travis, what if we left something open in Slattery Falls? A doorway to the afterlife or something like that?"

"Seems a bit dramatic."

"Do you have a better explanation?"

He didn't need to answer, but his face still appeared troubled. "Els, we can't just up and leave."

"Are you serious? It was your idea."

"And it was a bad one," he said. "I'm sorry. I was thinking out loud."

"One lead, one possibility to maybe find April, and you dig your heels in and say no?"

The reaction was unfair, of course, but I wanted to get my way, needed to get my way. Take back something that resembled control.

"Todd Benson," he said with a sigh. "We know what happened to him and who took him. But who did the town blame? Who did the neighborhood blame? The police, too, even if they didn't say it out loud?"

"Samantha and Michael, the parents. Shit."

"They both died never knowing what happened to Todd and being condemned for it on top of it all. The accusations build over time, especially when the parents hop in the car and leave town without telling anybody."

"So we tell them," I said.

"That we're going ghost hunting? That wasn't a bright thing to share even when the legalities were grayer. Now we're firmly in the realm of black and white."

I grabbed Travis' hands and squeezed. A shot of life to let him know I meant it and had no intention of fading back into the role of wraith I'd played for the last few days. "I made a mistake yesterday. We should be in Arizona by now, getting some rest in a run-down motel on the side of the road and safely outside the reach of that house, that monster. But we're not because I wouldn't let us leave. I'll be damned if I'm going to let that happen again. If you want to stay here and maintain innocence, be my guest, but I'm going with or without you."

Like me, approaching forty years old stole some of Travis' impulsive nature, so I gave him a moment, watched his eyes search the room as though one of the walls might hold the answer. They did, in a way. Framed photos of April, both alone and with us, lined the living room walls telling the story of her first five years and oddly reminiscent of the stations of the cross. A wet shine threatened to roll down his cheeks by the time his eyes looked over all there was to see. And I had my answer.

"I remember Slattery being a small town. Think there's anywhere to stay?" He tried to blink away the tears but only knocked them down like bowling pins.

"No idea, but I can think of someone who might."

CHAPTER SEVEN

Jeremiah Tedeschi answered the phone on the first ring. Evidently, the Slattery Falls Historical Society was still a one-man operation. He didn't introduce himself by name but his uppity tone reminded me of a clock wound to its breaking point. I hoped he wouldn't recognize my voice, especially since I had affected it with an awkward false bravado last time, but I imagine that day lived in his memory. Maybe the whole town celebrated the day the house came down.

"I'm not sure if you can help me, but I thought the historical society might be a good place to start."

"If I may be of assistance, I should be most happy to try." Not a chance he was smiling on the other end of the line.

"My husband and I are going to be traveling and were hoping to spend a night in Slattery Falls. We hoped to find some kind of accommodation within the town limits if possible."

"Ah, and your name, Miss?"

A surge of panic rose, making my heart beat a little too fast. I fought to keep the anxiety out of my words. "Costa," I said. "Elsie Costa." *Smooth, Elsie.* Maybe a little dramatic to give a fake name, but if the police decided to look for us, we didn't want to make their job too easy.

"Well, Ms. Costa, may I ask what brings you to our humble town?" A suspicious question asked without much suspicion. I recalled Tedeschi being a sourpuss, but still taking an immense amount of pride in his station. As such, I'd prepared for this question. A time existed when Slattery Falls eluded our detection. Until it didn't. Now you could plug it into any search engine and get results in spades. Including the world-renowned—or so their website claimed—Lang's Collective, which boasted an assortment of antique reamers that drew aficionados from near and far. Upon discovering the antique store, all I had to do was figure out what the hell a reamer was.

It makes juice, by the way. Especially useful if you have no access to a store that sells juice and want to build up your forearm muscles.

"Ah," came Tedeschi's response. "Of course. Well, I do wish you the utmost of luck in adding to your collection. Yes, I do believe we can find you a place to stay. Of course, you'll already know we are not a large town, and motels would be most...unbecoming. There are, however, several bed and breakfasts I'd be delighted to recommend." His voice transitioned to a conspiratorial whisper. "If you'd like, I could even call ahead and put in a word." If we were face-to-face, the man would have winked.

"Thank you, Mr. Tedeschi. My husband and I would appreciate that. Is there one you recommend over the others?"

"Yes..." He stretched the word to its breaking point. I grimaced, remembering he hadn't offered his name. The pause that followed seemed interminable, but he eventually must have concluded no foul play because when he spoke again, his tone lacked cynicism.

"They're all very cozy, top-notch facilities, but I daresay we should consider the Stone residence."

It took a moment to figure out why my stomach dropped so suddenly, though it should have been obvious. I'd read Emily Stone's diary, or at least the online approximation, cover to cover many times. Small town, my ass. This was too much to chalk up to coincidence.

"Ms. Costa? Are you there?"

"Yes, that will be fine. Just fine."

A few more formalities passed between us before Tedeschi gave me the phone number. Travis looked on with concern as I jotted down the digits on the back of an envelope. Bethany Stone. More than likely the great, great grand-something of Emily Stone, whose son vanished at the hands of Weeks. If a record existed of anyone finding the child's body, we never came across it. Did Bethany know about her lost relative? We had to figure out if we still had that ruthless cunning our younger selves possessed, because we needed every ounce of help to get April back.

Travis didn't comment, but his thoughts were etched across his face. He noticed the context clues, the pallor of my skin, my eyes like a scared rabbit, or some other tell I wasn't even aware of. He leaned in, noted the name on the envelope, and huffed.

"Jesus Christ, it never ends."

Bethany Stone exuded warmth over the phone, sprinkling in words like "dear" and "honey" wherever the conversation left space for them. She was a sea of tranquility in contrast to the fire of Emily's words. There were significantly fewer questions during this phone call, which only emphasized Tedeschi's impromptu background check. The man gave off a real "one of us" vibe.

Ms. Stone had an open room and could take us as soon as that night. We accepted, made sure she took cash, and set to packing.

We were eager to arrive in town before the sun went down. It was something of a tradition. Before we could leave, I had one last call to make. Maybe we'd luck out and the trip wouldn't be necessary.

The phone rang and rang until someone picked up with an audible click. A symphony of sound, voices shouting to be heard over a busy workplace, drowned out the answer on the other end of the line.

"Officer Metcalf?" I asked.

"Yes, how can I help you?"

I raised my voice, trying to keep frustration at bay. "Officer Metcalf, this is Elsie Morland."

"Elsie, hello! Hold on a moment, please." The clamor drifted into the background before a slamming door shut it off completely. My ears rang in the newfound silence. Metcalf cleared her throat and then spoke again. "How are you holding up?"

"I'm fine," I said, trying to inflect a smile into my voice. I let a beat pass, wondering why I felt the need to appear put together. "No, I'm not. I don't know why I said that. I'm not sleeping. I just… She's supposed to start school. Not until next fall, but we had registration scheduled. First week of November. What if she misses it?"

The words sounded so unimportant.

"I'm sorry," I said. "I only called to see if there were any updates, Officer."

"Call me, Robin," she said softly. "And there's no need to apologize, Mrs. Morland. Elsie. Can I call you Elsie?"

"Yes."

"Elsie, I wish I had an update to share with you. Please know that finding April is a top priority for this department. Every available officer is working on it. These are all people I trust." A moment passed. "I was going to call you today, actually."

My heart leaped. I yearned for any piece of news, no matter how trivial.

As if sensing my excitement, Robin added, "It may be a coincidence, but does the word 'weeks' hold any special significance?"

Time stopped. I don't know how long I held off answering, but the slam of the car trunk caught my attention. Travis had finished packing for the trip. I watched him out the window.

We have to call the police.

That's what he'd said.

Not because they can help us.

Because that's what people do.

I squashed down my panic, thankful Robin couldn't see how badly my hand trembled. "It's a fairly common word. I'm not sure it holds any special meaning for me. I can ask Travis, if you like."

"No, no. That's okay. Probably nothing," she said. "We interviewed a man—not a person of interest, airtight alibi—but we found an item in his store. A similar doll to the one hidden under April's window."

"Where did he get it?" I whispered.

"Well, that's the thing. We're not sure," said Robin. "He's only been able to say one word."

"Weeks. What do you mean 'been able'?"

Robin cleared her throat. "I'm afraid I can't share that. You're correct, though. About the word. Strange, but probably unrelated. Nonetheless, something we will keep our eyes on. Listen, Elsie, I'm booked up today, but maybe I could stop by tomorrow. Talk a little more about this?"

"We, uh, we won't be here."

"I'm sorry?" Robin's warm tone faltered for a second before returning with extra saccharine. "Can you tell me where you'll be? In case we need to contact you urgently."

"Travis' parents," I lied. "In Connecticut. We just need a little… support, you know?"

The hard-nosed detective disappeared as the woman who had won April over emerged. "Of course. How long will you be away?"

"A night or two."

A pencil scratched paper on the other end of the line. "Okay, I'll be in touch if anything comes of the 'weeks' connection we discussed. Or if anything else comes to light. Call me any time, day or night."

"Thank you so much, Robin." A grimy feeling washed over me as I hung up.

"Shit," I whispered. Travis came back inside to find me rubbing my eyes.

"What is it?" he said as he looked at the phone in my hand.

"He's back."

CHAPTER EIGHT

With no time to waste, I filled Travis in as we drove. When I finished giving the details of Robin's phone call, silence overtook the interior of our little sedan.

Route 84 carried us to 90. We'd hopped in the car of our own volition, but that didn't eliminate the feeling of being dragged, held captive. As we merged onto Route 91, more than halfway through the short trip, the air grew heavier inside the car and my heart sank whenever I glanced at the empty backseat. The expectation of dark clouds rolling in, pregnant with lightning and ready to cast enough rain to necessitate a second ark, stood vivid in my mind. But the sun shone and the clouds kept their distance.

Nerves fluttered through my body as the exit numbers ascended, drawing us closer to our destination. We turned the radio on, found nothing to distract us, and shut it off again. Repeat ad nauseum. I smiled at Travis, an attempt to alleviate some of the tension, and hoped my effort appeared a little less fake than the smile it received in return.

Exit 25 - Northampton

"Where do we start?" I asked, unable to bear the silence any longer.

"The rubble, I guess. The whole thing collapsed like a house of fuckin' cards, so I don't know what exactly there'll be to find, but there's got to be something to go off there. A clue, if you will."

"Not bad enough that this whole charade started off with ghost hunting, now we're playing Sherlock Holmes." Travis was good enough to force a laugh, but it held no humor.

Exit 26 - Hadley

Trees passed. Mile markers passed. A roadside shrine to a lost life passed.

Exit 27 - Whately

"What if the answer isn't there?" I blurted out. "You really think it could be as easy as turning over a pile of crushed house and finding April, smile on her face, ready to go home?"

"I don't think that at all. I think we don't have anything else to go on. If we don't hold out hope that there's someone or something in that town that could lead us to her, we might as well turn around and go home. Sit in the living room with thumbs up our asses and wait."

Exit 32 - North Hatfield

Tears rose to the surface. I tried to choke them down so hard my throat ached. He was blunt, but he was right. The only path forward lay overgrown, and not with just any kind of flora and fauna. Toxic plantlife riddled with sharp thorns, small so you don't notice them until they've wheedled their way under your skin and taken root. This way lies infection.

I shook my head to clear it. "You're right." I tried not to sound choked up. "There's nothing back there."

"I don't know that I'd put it like that—"

"Nope, it's true. I can feel it. Any future this family has goes through Slattery Falls. It's like… destiny, almost."

"Destiny," he said, trying on the word like a new pair of shoes. No bias, no judgment in the way he presented it. Almost like he was willing to believe it but had yet to wrap his mind around the concept.

"Maybe that's not the right word, but it's the first that comes to mind."

Exit 34 - Deerfield

"Weeks said he chose us," I said.

Travis shuddered, small but undeniable. "Are you sure it's wise to say that name given where we're going?"

I narrowed my eyes at him. He kept his on the road, pretending not to notice. "He's not fucking Voldemort, Travis."

He lifted a hand from the wheel and waved it as if to say *fair point.*

Exit 35 - Conway

"Weeks chose us, some bullshit about knowing you and I would end up together before we'd even met. He never elaborated on it. What made us so powerful that he had to lure us in for like half our lives?" I asked. "Didn't you ever wonder?"

"Of course." He shrugged. "I almost brought it up half-a-dozen times, but it seemed—I don't know—taboo. Like that was all behind us and it was better left in the past. Talking about it would only bring up painful memories."

"Maybe it's the wrong read, but I don't think Slattery Falls and Robert Weeks were ever truly in the rearview mirror. You ever have a day go by you don't think about it?"

He shook his head, eyes locked on the road ahead.

"Me either," I said. "Then there's the nightmares."

Exit 36 - Hobson

"So what does it all mean?"

I let out a chuckle. Couldn't help it. "Absolutely fucked if I know. But maybe, just maybe, as much as I've beaten myself up for not getting directly in the car and booking it out of state, that doesn't matter. What if we were always meant to come back here?"

He'd been staring straight ahead for most of the drive, but now his eyes moved up to the right, taking in the bright green exit sign, then turning to me. A subtle movement of his left hand set the metronomic click of the turn signal in motion.

Exit 37 - Slattery Falls

"I guess we'll find out," he said.

Travis didn't slow at all as the exit approached, and for a second I thought he would drive right past. He looked at me, held my gaze, then sighed as his eyes moved back to the road. With a jerk of the wheel we left the highway and took the exit that led to Slattery Falls.

CHAPTER NINE

During our last trip, Slattery Falls itself was no more than window dressing, a nondescript curtain that hid the ugliness of the Weeks House. The house, or what remained of it, was stop number one, but how far could a pile of rubble really go in helping us locate April?

A gas station sat at the base of the exit ramp, overgrown by unkempt shrubbery and decorated by graffiti and broken windows. Someone could've torn it down a long time ago, but instead it persisted as a sign encouraging travelers to get back on the highway. Whatever you came for, you won't find it here. Evidently a two-bit historical society could only do so much.

A single road snaked past the gas station, leading us into the town proper. At the road's entry point stood a weather-worn sign welcoming us to Slattery Falls. Some folks might call the sign rustic, but decayed was probably a better fit.

The pall I expected to find hanging over the town kept to the shadows and the dilapidated fashion of the gas station stayed relegated to the highway exit. Everything along the town's main stretch appeared almost cozy. Don't get me wrong, it still felt like a trap—outstretched talons waiting just down the mouth of the closest alley to reach out and grab unsuspecting victims. The store windows, however, brimmed with displays painstakingly crafted by Mom and Pop shopkeepers. It all screamed 1950s television.

Meter-free parking spots jutted out diagonally along the sidewalks, which contained a healthy flow of people. Parents and children with carefree smiles plastered on their faces traversed the streets, unrushed. Add in a little unseasonal snow and you would have had a Hallmark Christmas movie. Was it possible to live in Slattery Falls and not know the history? Even more pertinent, was it possible to know the history and ignore it?

I couldn't wrap my head around the idea, but then again, my head hadn't been in the best shape for the last few days. Truth be told, I wasn't even sure what day of the week it was.

"Must be the weekend," said Travis, as if hearing my thoughts. "Kids would be in school otherwise." He inclined his head toward the car's LED display, 12:03 in neon green.

"It's peaceful," I said. "I guess I didn't expect that."

"I remember this place, or at least aspects of it, being perfectly peaceful on the surface, then telling a very different story once we got underground."

"Point. Still..."

"Hey, Lang's Collective," said Travis, gesturing at a storefront. "Try and remember that."

Sure enough, the massive display window boasted a collection of small ceramic dishes with a rounded center poking out. Why anyone would need more than one old-fashioned juicer was beyond me. Collectors gonna collect.

I studied the display through the crowd of people. A woman leading a small child by the hand—no older than April—stopped in front of the collective and glared toward our car. Her face displayed a frown that held more anger than confusion or sadness. The first hint of unfriendliness in this otherwise idyllic town struck me as strange.

Then her eyes flashed green.

It happened in under a second, a blaze of emerald fire. The woman's eyes returned to a normal hue as a smile traced its way back onto her lips. The little girl tugged her hand and they continued on their way.

My heart pounded as I spun around to follow their progress, twisting myself into my seatbelt, but they vanished into a cluster of pedestrians.

"What the fuck?" I whispered, drawing a concerned look from Travis.

"You okay, Els?"

"My eyes are playing tricks on me, I think."

He turned to me, silently asking for more, but I forced a smile and assured him everything was okay. His furrowed brows told me he didn't buy it.

As my heartbeat slowed, Travis eased the car past a pharmacy, a secondhand bookstore, a bakery, a deli, no less than ten different restaurants, and various other shops one expected to see on the type of Main Street that necessitates a speed limit of fifteen miles per hour. Travis had a heavy foot, and I knew it was hard for him to keep the car crawling along. We'd grown used to the more eastern part of Massachusetts where people drove fifty through the center of town and responded with a single finger if you didn't like it.

Before the last business gave way to a residential area of town, Travis pointed out the office of the Slattery Falls Historical Society. A single man toiled away at a desk, his back facing the window. He didn't need to turn around for us to guess who it was, whiling away his afternoon in a small plain office like Bob Cratchit on Christmas Eve.

"We'll have to stop in and see him before we leave," I said, part jest and part residual guilt.

Travis kept quiet. His eyes were fixed on the fork in the road ahead. To the right, small suburban neighborhoods housed the residents of Slattery Falls, including Bethany Stone. To the left, there wasn't much to see, but the negative space stood out as the first patch of dark storm clouds on an otherwise sunny day. In a monster movie, maybe one with vampires, the camera would pan to the twisted stretch of road that takes our protagonist to the cursed castle. As the audience lays eyes on this haunted structure for the first time, a crack of thunder assaults the eardrums and lightning flashes in the sky. An ill omen.

Down the left-hand road, the castle no longer stood, but the path leading to its ruins appeared as foreboding as ever.

Travis took his foot off the gas and let the car coast so slowly that when it stopped, it took a moment to realize the car was no longer in motion. Our Toyota waited at the nexus of a crossroads, the weight of decision heavy on our shoulders.

"This is why we came," Travis whispered. The words hung in the air, followed by a sigh. "Imagine if all it took was a short drive up that road."

"We don't have a plan."

"We didn't have a fucking plan last time."

"And you haven't gotten any less salty about that." I gave him a half-grin to let him know I wasn't serious. "We *did* have a Josh last time. That's as good as having two or three more hands on deck."

A blaring honk made us both jump and nearly bash our heads on the ceiling. Not everybody around here exhibited a Pleasantville level of friendliness, it seemed. Travis moved his foot from the brake to the gas and turned the car right. We weren't ready to face the house quite yet.

CHAPTER TEN

We knew Bethany Stone's address, sure enough, but hadn't made it to this end of town on our last trip. Trying to find the bed and breakfast reminded me of a family vacation, except in the good old days we didn't have a woman's electronic voice dictating each turn.

Travis and I had rushed to get out of the house, lest Officer Robin decide she had time to drop in after all. Red-eyed and functioning only on caffeine and adrenaline, we wouldn't have held up under pressure. All that to say, researching Slattery Falls' variety of bed and breakfasts to make sure we didn't get put in the creepy doll room, or have to use a shared bathroom ranked pretty low on our list of things to do.

Not that Bethany Stone's glorified cottage was a hovel by any definition of the word, but it was small. Not more than two bedrooms, a living room, and likely a shared bathroom, judging from the outside. Like it or not, it seemed like even if we only stayed one night, we'd get to know Ms. Stone intimately. If she was half as helpful as her relative, I could live with that.

We turned onto Fox Street. The GPS told us we'd arrived as we pulled up to the third house on the left. Travis parked the car and sat back, eyes still pointed forward as though waiting for more instructions. I could have used that outside interference myself. Thankfully, neither of us had to demonstrate free will. The front door of the cottage flew open, like the plump older woman in a night dress who now filled the frame had kicked it before barreling outside. If the smiles on Main Street were unsettling, this woman's grin inspired sheer terror.

Or maybe we just weren't used to people being happy to see us.

I tore my eyes away from our host and found Travis already looking at me, a mixture of worry and amusement on his face. "This could actually be fun."

It was the wrong thing to say, but I'll be damned if I didn't laugh a little. We opened the doors and stood by the car, waiting for the rampaging woman to amble down the walk and make our acquaintance. She got Travis first, wrapping him in an embrace that would've cracked one of my ribs. He caught my eye from over her shoulder, wincing in pain. Letting him down, she turned to me next but took it easier. At least she didn't lift me off the ground.

"Jesus please us, it's so good to have you here. I'm Bethany. And well, I'm sure you guessed it, but this is where you'll be staying." She stepped back and held an arm out to present the cottage, a ringmaster displaying their wide array of acts.

Travis clapped. God help me, he clapped.

"Well, don't be shy," Bethany added. "Let me help you with your things. Let's get you inside."

"No worries, Ms. Stone. We packed light," said Travis.

"Oh, call me Beth, please. We'll be bunking up after all."

Between Travis' applause and now the look of abject horror at the notion of bunking up with this kooky old woman, I couldn't hold back a laugh. I tried to stifle it, but couldn't keep the damn thing inside. I didn't intend it to be cruel, and judging by the way Bethany—Beth—joined in, I don't think that's how she took it. This woman was, simply put, the furthest thing from what I expected to burst through the door and welcome us to this wretched town. Another laugh escaped, this one bringing a tear with it.

"Forgive me, Beth," I said. "Long trip and we're a little tired for it."

"Of course, dear. Mind if I call you Elsie?" she asked, leading me by the elbow toward the front door. Travis slammed the trunk and followed with the bags.

"Not at all."

"I do love that name. You don't hear it much anymore. It was my husband's grandmother's name, you know."

My feet quit working and Beth nearly lost her footing when my elbow stopped following along. "Was it really?"

"Yes," she said, slow and careful, unsure what to make of my excessive interest. I shook the strange reaction off and filed the information away. Likely a coincidence, but until April was safe, we couldn't afford to believe in those.

We stepped inside the house. The smell of cinnamon swirling around with a touch of vanilla overwhelmed me. Either Beth had baked in preparation for our arrival, or she kept up one of those stereotypical grandmother-type places.

"Any idea how long you'll be staying, dearie?"

I looked to Travis. He shook his head in an unhelpful manner, so I answered. "At least the night. Maybe longer if…"

Eyes widened slightly, Beth gave me room to finish the sentence, then took care of it for me when I couldn't. "If you don't find what you're looking for?"

"Yes," I said, suddenly fighting tears. "We're looking for something very important."

She nodded as if she understood completely. "Antiques, wasn't it?"

A hard swallow. "Yes." A little more firmness behind it this time. "Travis and I would love nothing more than to find what we came for as soon as possible. Maybe even this afternoon. But that could just be senseless optimism."

Beth didn't answer right away, perhaps detecting a hint of sadness that didn't have anything to do with the reamer-that-got-away. When she did speak, her voice was soft. "I don't book in advance. I suspect that's why Jeremiah recommended me, so you're welcome to stay as long as you need."

"Thank you," I said, putting on a smile that I hoped looked genuine. I don't know how close I came to pulling it off.

"Well," she said, letting out a deep breath. Perkiness seeped back into her voice. "Let me show you around. You can see the living room, of course. You're welcome to use the television anytime you like. Except for Friday and Sunday nights. That's my *Dateline* time. I never miss a night with Keith Morrison." She whispered the last part like a secret.

Travis and I nodded, not sure what was an appropriate reply to a wacky old woman sharing a celebrity crush. She beckoned us toward the hallway. I wasn't longing for the grimy, stained sheets at a roadside motel, but some middle ground must exist between that and the spare bedroom we walked into.

Sunlight poured in a single open window, making the colors pop on a homemade quilt. The queen-size bed took up over half the room. A mountain of throw pillows covered the bed's surface area and I already dreaded finding a place to put them all when it came time to sleep. A weathered dresser held three jars of homemade potpourri, a collection of pinecones and pine needles jammed in a blender to overpower the room with nature's pungent musk.

"Well, what do you think?" Beth grinned expectantly.

"We love it," said Travis. He slipped an arm around my shoulder and pulled me close to sell it.

She squealed, punctuating the noise with a short series of claps. "Wonderful! Have you had lunch?"

We hadn't. Interrupting the trip up 91 north didn't occur to us, and as welcoming as Bethany had been so far, we didn't want to put her out.

"Yes," I lied, "but thank you. I think we'll take a few minutes to settle in if that's okay."

"Of course, dear. Of course! I'll leave you to it."

She bounced down the hall, dress trailing behind her. The hollow in my chest ached thinking of April, but an innate feeling, combined with Travis' goofy grin as he watched her go, told me we were exactly where we needed to be at the moment.

CHAPTER ELEVEN

Opening our suitcases revealed little more than just how quickly we'd rushed to pack and get out. Stupid things like having enough t-shirts to last a month but only one pair of pants, toothpaste but no toothbrushes, and an odd number of socks. This was how unsupervised children filled a suitcase. Or parents whose exhausted minds wandered elsewhere.

We didn't bother unpacking into the potpourri-lined dresser. Instead, we left the bags on the floor, went back out into the living room and did our best to look like antique hunters, and not two terrified parents hoping to find the only thing that gave the world any meaning. Bethany looked over the top of her Hap and Leonard mystery and smiled so big her lips smacked. She went back to her book as we ducked out the front door and waved goodbye. Either we'd executed the ploy to perfection or appeared too maniacal to bother with. The poor woman likely regretted taking on the headcases in her guestroom. I just hoped she wouldn't assume we'd escaped from some kind of institution and call the police.

Fox Street led out to Solomon Way before that dropped us back at the fateful fork in the road. The path to the house looked as ominous as it had earlier, but this time no traffic waited to be let by. The area was deserted, the kind of place that made pedestrians take the long way home without realizing why. It gave us all the time in the world to wait around imagining worst-case scenarios before making the inevitable decision.

Travis must have felt that pressure, but he didn't show it. He made a flawless U-turn onto the unmarked road. My hand hovered over my pocket as I debated pulling up the maps app and trying to figure out the name of the road. A metal pole split the corner, teeming with rust, but a resident had removed the sign at some point. Whether it was a conscientious elder trying to bury the Weeks House in the annals of forgotten history or a teenager with a penchant for local lore was up for debate. I suspected the former but hoped for the latter. As long as the people, youth or otherwise, spoke of Robert Weeks, they'd never truly forget what that monster, and others like him, were capable of.

Branches lay scattered across the road in various states of decay.

Between dodging those and potholes, Travis had his hands full. The sight was at odds with the otherwise clear roads we'd encountered throughout the rest of town. The body appeared healthy, even if the heart did not.

Despite the recent Nor'easter, these branches and the other debris did not appear new to the area. It had gathered over the years, a result of the town withdrawing itself from the looming shadow of that hateful house.

My heart beat just above a healthy clip as our silver sedan sped toward the site of the house. The farther we pulled up the incline, the madder I became, almost hoping to round a corner and see every inch of that bearded fuck blocking our path. He would beam, thinking he got the best of us, had stolen the most important people in our lives twice now, but dead, undead, or banished to some otherworldly realm, I'd tear him apart or die trying.

"Whoa. You okay?" asked Travis. Concern dotted his eyes. "You're breathing pretty heavy."

My lips started to form the words *I'm fine* before I pulled them back, kept them from reaching the one person in the universe I didn't need to pretend with.

"Far from it," I laughed. My breathing slowed. "It's got to be the... I don't know, the atmosphere here, I guess." I let Travis think through the implication before asking the next question. "Is it getting to you at all?"

"No," he said, an answer that should have inspired confidence, should have made him appear ready to charge forth into battle. But the word shook. He spoke it in the tone of a child tugging at the sleeve of a mall security guard to inquire about their missing parents. He continued, "I don't feel much of anything. I feel shielded, but that almost makes it sound positive. Maybe numb would be a better description." He took a deep breath. "I don't like it, Els. I don't know what to make of it."

Before I could make a guess, we pulled around a tight curve and arrived at the base of the hill where the Weeks House had stood. Yellow police tape crisscrossed the road in front of us, keeping us from encroaching on the house's land, even if only via symbolism.

Travis put the car in park and turned the key, letting the engine falter then die, leaving only a rapidly fading series of clicks in the otherwise silent afternoon air. Parking the car in the middle of the road felt irresponsible, but the littered debris told us if no one had cleared the road in five years, they weren't about to start today. I pushed the door behind me harder than I meant to. It slammed shut with a loud boom and I nearly jumped out of my skin. I jerked my head around to catch Travis' look, daring him to laugh, but he didn't. The same immature little boy who never met a tense life-or-death situation he couldn't think up a smartass comment for suddenly didn't find life so funny. He shifted his ring up and down his fourth finger as he stared at his feet.

I turned back toward the tape and felt as though a weight tugged down on my chin, trying to keep me from seeing the horror ahead. I didn't expect to see Weeks. Rather I knew the house would be there, climbing to the sky, reformed through a combination of magic and hatred, living only to steal from the residents of this poor little town whose only crime was existence. I saw the gothic mansion clear as day in my mind, every window filled with green eyes, the color of sea glass but not nearly as tranquil.

My eyes met only open air. The idea of the house rising from the ashes wasn't something my already dwindling sanity could deal with. Of the many things I'll never forget from that warm August afternoon five years back, one stands out the clearest. Travis and I held hands as Weeks' evil consumed the structure from the inside out, burying the body of our friend. Our family. Celebration and mourning aren't mutually exclusive—how many times have you heard others speaking of celebrating someone's life at a funeral?—but that moment painted the perfect picture of how the two could walk hand in hand. Even replaying the events in my mind, time slowed and the ethereal guitar riff from The Pixies' "Where is my Mind?" played softly in the background.

Like the road leading up to it, the pile of rubble hadn't changed much in the intervening years. If people had come and gone, they had followed the old adage of taking only pictures and leaving only footprints.

"How's it feel?" asked Travis, pulling me away from my thoughts.

"Positively surreal." I laughed and brushed a strand of hair away behind my ear, a telltale motion that screamed *Please don't think I'm crazy.* "This is going to sound ridiculous. For a minute there, I really expected it to have rebuilt itself."

"Not ridiculous," he said, shaking his head.

"You, too?"

"Yeah." An uneasy tone overtook his voice.

I took the first step over the yellow tape and walked toward the gaping mound of refuse. Travis followed, releasing a sigh of relief that I'd taken the initiative. Boldness didn't enter into it, only time. Weeks had taken April and if this shithole turned out to be a dead end, better we find out sooner rather than later.

Gates, I thought with a sudden jolt of panic. *Hadn't Tedeschi unlocked the gates for us last time?*

I spun around, searching the area where domesticated land met forest, but saw nothing, even down to the car and beyond.

"There should at least be holes where the fence stood, right? Shards of metal that made up the gates, blown to bits by the force of the implosion?"

Travis joined me spinning in circles, gawping like a wide-eyed fish. "Jesus, I didn't even think of it."

"They're gone. Like the land… devoured them."

He narrowed his eyes and scrunched up one side of his face. "We shouldn't get worked up about it. There are too many reasonable explanations. It could be buried under all the other shit for all we know."

"I just—"

"I'm not discounting things disappearing and moving of their own accord around here. My memory isn't that short. But I don't see why he would make the fence disappear. What does he gain?"

"That's what scares me. We just got here and already things aren't where they're supposed to be." Goosebumps formed on the back of my arm as I said it.

"We'll keep an eye out," said Travis, turning that weird scrunch into something like a smile. It made me grimace more than it made me want to return the look.

Shards of wood, broken glass, cement blocks, window shutters, and roof tiles composed endless piles, making the land look like an explosion at a city dump. Indoor commodities like furniture, paintings, and rugs caught my eye, appearing almost uncomfortable outside of their natural environment.

As I approached the pile that used to be the front door, led home by the litter-strewn walkway, a glint of metal caught my eye. Much of the heap glittered like gold, but this piece shared the same hue as the fabled metal. I picked it up.

I quickly identified it as the knocker we'd found fixed to the front door on our previous visit. We hadn't tried it out, less out of fear, and more because the house's occupant already knew of our arrival. No house stood before us now, but that only meant the evil was no longer contained. It still knew we'd arrived.

An agonizing shock pulsed through me and I dropped the lion-head knocker into a pile of glass shards with a staccato crunch, lost beneath the sound of my own shriek.

The lion's eyes.

They'd turned green for a split second, and in that time they studied me, quietly laughing at the futility of all this. Revelation upon revelation entered my mind, each one more upsetting than the last.

She belongs to me now.

She's finally home.

Maybe she'll get to meet her uncle.

You. Will. Never. Find. Her.

You. Will. Never—

"Find her." April whispered the last two words, her face emblazoned over the lion's head of the knocker. She stared up at me from the pile of glass, dark circles around her eyes. A hint of green glimmered in each pupil, growing larger and larger, charging forward like a freight train. The glow became too bright to look at. I squinted and began to turn away when her visage burst into a cloud of light then disappeared as quickly as it had formed.

My head cracked forward as the barrage of cruel words returned, marching through my head like a parade and accompanied by a hellish laughter I knew all too well. Laughter and screaming mingled together to form an orchestral arrangement for the damned. The cacophony grew and grew, pressure building inside my head until I knew it must explode.

Only when I forced my eyes open did the scream stop. My throat stung as Travis raced toward me, and my cheeks reddened as I figured out where the scream came from. His hands rested on my shoulders, trying to bring me back from the daze that cursed object had brought on.

"Don't touch anything," I choked out between sobs.

His eyes found the door knocker on the ground and he kept any follow-up questions to himself. Travis knelt and scooped me up in his arms. I didn't remember falling down. I couldn't have lost more than a few seconds, but the knocker had stolen that time from me nonetheless.

Minutes passed as Travis rubbed my shoulders, whispering softly in an attempt to calm me down. When I regained enough composure to look up at him without bawling uncontrollably again, he asked, "What happened?"

I told him everything I remembered. Everything.

When I'd finished, his already pale skin tone had blanched a shade or two closer to bone white. I didn't ask if he believed me. That question didn't exist between us anymore. Travis Morland could rattle off any story, no matter how far-fetched, and my response would be to ask "What are we going to do about it?". So when Elsinore Morland told him a haunted doorknob broke her brain, he nodded with lips set in a straight line and said, "What do we do next?"

The small gesture nearly reduced me to tears again.

"We can't give up, and it can't all be touched by evil. I refuse to believe the mad motherfucker put a hex on every brick."

"Husky?"

I shook my head, allowing the ghost of a smile to touch my lips. Fifteen years and countless explorations, we'd never officially gone through with a "husky", our confirmation that enough was enough and we needed to get out, consequences be damned.

"It's there if we need it." Travis' soft tone gave way as his eyes shot open nearly as wide as his mouth. Scrambling backward, he tripped over a splintered board that may have belonged to the porch at one time.

Trusting his ass to cushion his fall, I looked over my shoulder and immediately wished I hadn't. A cloaked figure leaned out from behind a large oak. It wore no trench coat, so it wasn't one of the workers from my dream. A hood kept their face in shadow, except for two shimmering green eyes. The same as April in my vision. The same as the woman from town.

The figure remained statue-like, perhaps not yet understanding that we'd seen them. Travis scrabbled to his feet and held out an arm to shield me. Keeping his eyes on the figure, he leaned over and picked up a weathered old board, about the length of his arm and no longer as firm as it once had been, but still better than nothing.

He charged and the hooded person darted into the dark depths of the woods. My heart plummeted as Travis disappeared after it, screaming obscenities. Despite the day's relative warmth, I shivered with him out of sight. I expected a trap. With my husband lured away, a dozen of those emerald-eyed beasts would appear from thin air and steal me away. Cold sweat trickled down my back at the thought, quickly replaced by an odd sense of hope. Maybe they would take me away to April.

I closed my eyes and waited for them to come.

CHAPTER TWELVE

I sat in the middle of the debris waiting for Travis to return. The crunch of autumn leaves made my eyes shoot wide open, but nothing was there except a soft breeze. The sun hovered over the treeline, providing just enough light to ensure I was still alone.

More crunching came from the solid darkness that lived between each trunk.

"Travis," I called, more a hope than an affirmation.

A pair of green lights stared back at me then vanished as quickly as they'd appeared. Another pair illuminated, glaring out from across the grove before blinking into darkness once more. Nothing emerged from the woods, but the eyes traveled from one copse to the next with impossible speed. Impossible for a single person, at least. The sound of leaves crackling underfoot disappeared momentarily as the lights continued peeking out around me faster than I could turn my head to meet them. When the footsteps returned, they grew louder and louder, coming directly at me. My heart pounded as I braced for a robed figure to burst from the darkness, revealed in all its horrifying glory under the dying sunlight.

My panic stilled when Travis emerged, huffing and puffing. With twigs decorating his hair, he helped me to my feet. I shook my head, half hoping to find myself back home with April lining up another cannonball aimed at the center of our bed. Give me every "it was all a dream" trope mashed together. I would graciously accept any and all of them.

"Didn't catch them?"

He shook his head, still winded.

"Not Weeks, though."

"I don't think so," he panted. "Too short. Not bulky enough. Weeks was six feet and change even before he pulled a Paul Bunyan on us."

"That's worse," I said, feeling the hair on the back of my neck stand at attention. "That means he's working with someone." The green dots danced in my memory. "Maybe multiple someones. I only got a quick glimpse, but it wasn't one of the workers that helped build the place. Right?"

"Can't be sure," he said, but I think he was.

We wandered the property for more than an hour, never losing sight of each other. Taking care not to put our hands on anything else that might trigger an episode, we scoured the remains of the Weeks House. Charred paper amid ravaged bindings told us one particular heap held the remains of the library, perhaps burned by people trying to execute what their forebears couldn't. This town had tried to extinguish Weeks' legacy, allowing fire to consume anything in its path. The stories told of how fire couldn't touch the house itself, or at least couldn't survive for long, but once the belongings made their way to free Slattery Falls air, all bets were off.

A single book lay untouched by flame, sheltered away from other burned volumes and broken bookshelves. I stumbled back like it was a snake curled in the grass, and though I caught a hungry look in Travis' eye, I shook my head and mouthed the words *don't you dare touch it.* My head still spun from getting handsy with Weeks' belongings.

It wasn't until we found the ruins of the servant's kitchen that we discovered the first item of interest—the entrance to the basement. Crumbled brick lined the hole in the ground that dropped to the purgatory beneath. I wondered why the familiar force would draw us here, to re-enter the place that housed our worst memories and go toe to toe in a rematch. When we approached, we saw the futility in that line of thought. The moldering stairs descended only a few feet before stone, brick, and wood debris overtook them in staggering amounts.

I knelt and touched a single finger to the top step, half expecting another shock to the system, but the stone felt lifeless. I can't explain it any better than that. Upon entering the Weeks House with Travis and Josh, we'd all felt watched before even stepping foot inside. That feeling no longer existed. Nothing lived in the remains of the house. It was free now.

"Let's go," I said, standing. I shook my finger to get rid of any emotional residue from the structure.

"You didn't get a key, did you?" I whispered. The sun kissed the horizon, and though the day still had a little life left, barging into the house seemed in poor taste.

Travis shook his head and reached for the knob. It turned in his hand and the door gave way. The picturesque downtown that met us upon our arrival returned to mind. Of course, Slattery Falls was the kind of place where people didn't lock their doors. I stopped my eyes from rolling and stepped over the threshold. Raucous snoring filled the living room, rising to such decibels it seemed to shake the picture frames on the walls. Travis eased the door shut to avoid disturbing Bethany's afternoon siesta, but when the latch clicked gently shut, her slumped form shot forward in the recliner, launching her book to the floor. My heart nearly leapt from my mouth.

"Oh my. My, my, my. I must have dozed off there for a bit." She popped to her feet and frantically straightened her dress. "Well, I don't see any bags. Am I to take it your search was in vain?"

I couldn't answer. Thankfully, Travis pulled my feet from the fire.

"No luck today, Ms. Stone. But we'll carry on, try again tomorrow."

"Carry on," she repeated as though she didn't understand. "Of course. Well, I do wish you the best of luck. And please, call me Beth." She retrieved her book from the floor, marked her page, and placed it on an end table.

"Beth, then," said Travis.

"Good. Now, who's hungry?"

Bethany Stone served up homemade clam chowder that tasted better than any restaurant on Cape Cod ever dreamt of. A few bottles of amber ale each, from a local brewery in Edmond, hit the spot, and while the drinks couldn't wash away the failures of the day, they brought the night on a little faster. I could deal with that. I studied the bottle, felt its icy perspiration against my hands. I don't think I'd ever been to Edmond with Travis, but I could picture it spelled out on an exit sign.

We made small talk, sticking close to our real lives, but remembering to answer to Costa whenever Bethany forgot her own rules about informality. Overall, the evening was pleasant, and while a little eccentric, Bethany Stone possessed a good heart. Having lost her husband a decade prior, she began her own business to target the two things she loved in life: having company and providing comfort for others. Even with the warm fuzziness of the ale wrapping around my brain, a small panic surged in the back of my mind. The one question she could ask to derail the evening.

How come a lovely couple like you two doesn't have any kids?

But it never came.

"So, Bethany... Beth," said Travis with the confidence only a light buzz can provide. "Tell us a little about Slattery Falls. History and whatnot."

A dark cloud passed across her features, so brief I might have imagined it. Only I hadn't, and the notion sobered me up. I sat forward, anxious to see what Travis had up his sleeve.

"What do you want to know?" asked Bethany. I might have missed the careful change in her tone if I weren't listening for it.

"Well, downtown seems wonderful. Kind of a throwback to the halcyon days. I don't remember seeing a single chain there. All Mom and Pop."

A twinkle returned to her eye as the conversation strolled down innocent avenues. "Yes, I mentioned Jeremiah before, but the town's historical society does do quite a bit of legwork to keep the corporations from moving in, and of course they'd love to. We're not so far from Worcester, you know."

"And of course, the houses are beautiful," he continued, swirling a nearly empty bottle as he spoke. "Very… I don't know if traditional is the right word, but there's a classical style present in the homes, the road, even the mailboxes for goodness' sake."

Fifteen years spent together and I'd heard my share of "fuck's sake" and "Christ's sake", but never "for goodness' sake". My interest was piqued.

"And this cottage fits the town's style."

"If I didn't know better, Mr. Costa, I'd think you were trying to butter an old woman up. You don't seem to be asking a question so much as offering an endless parade of compliments."

Travis was silent for a moment, which he emphasized by ceasing the movement of his bottle. He took a sip before continuing, draining the dregs. "We got turned around coming back from the antique store. Took a road that led us up a hill and was all taped off. It kind of looked like a crime scene, if I'm honest."

Beth didn't answer, so Travis gave her a nudge.

"We were curious, so we got out of the car and took a look around. It looked for all the world like the foundation of a house. But like the whole damn thing just up and went kablooey. BAM!" He pounded the bottle on the table. "Wood and bricks everywhere. So I guess my question, Beth, is in a town this lovely, what's the deal with an eyesore like that?"

Beth stared him down and Travis met her gaze, nothing hostile, more like two chess players sizing one another up. They'd both forgotten about my presence or as good as.

"Why do I get the feeling you already know this story?" she whispered.

"We're but two weary travelers looking for antique… something," he finished weakly.

"Reamers," I added, making them both jump and effectively destroying our weak-as-shit cover story.

She narrowed her eyes, assessing us as if for the first time. "Who are you?"

CHAPTER THIRTEEN

Thank goodness we ate dinner on the early side because the conversation stretched late into the night. We told her about April, and how we assumed a false identity to slip out of Southbridge and avoid suspicion. Beth nearly choked on her drink when Josh's part of the story came up, and we credited him as the main reason the Weeks House no longer burdened Slattery Falls. Honestly, I think that last bit earned us some brownie points.

What inspired the unprompted flow of honesty? I can't pin it down. Maybe it was the higher-than-average proof of Edmond's Amber Ale, maybe it was Travis slipping effortlessly into a persona he hadn't employed since Josh was alive, a reminder of simpler times before life weighed heavy on his shoulders. If forced to choose one option, I'd say we trusted Bethany. Emily Stone and I lived more than a century apart, and yet I felt a kinship with her. If anyone could understand, it was Bethany.

After Travis and I laid our cards on the table, Bethany put down her own hand.

She had married into the Stone family, but that didn't make her any less a part of it. Her father-in-law, Burt, used to tell her stories about the Slattery Falls disappearances when the hour grew late and his glass clinked, not enough liquid left to keep the ice cubes from knocking together. He told Beth the stories in the light of a slowly dying fire. Her husband, Aaron—"God rest his soul," she added—had heard them all, of course. Burt used to treat his son to real-life horror as morality tales during Aaron's childhood. Yet even as an adult, he hung on his father's every word. So did Beth.

It seemed as though Emily and Burt weren't the only storytellers in the Stone lineage. With daylight long gone and drinks dwindling, Beth launched into the tale.

One night, Burt offered Beth a new story—the time the town caught the monster. The boogeyman, a pure manifestation of evil, walked among shadows for years, snatching children from the grip of their parents, creeping up to their windows at night in hopes they'd open the pane. Just a crack would do. And if they didn't, Robert Weeks would get them anyway.

Burt appeared uneasy as he spoke, and he shelved his usual flourishes for a hardline, factual type of storytelling. More like he was reading from the newspaper than spinning a yarn. He took no pleasure in it. Aaron's eyes contained no surprise, no wonder. He'd heard this one before, knew how the story ended. No surprise there. None of Burt's stories ever drew anything but rapt attention from him, even on the hundredth retelling, but that night was different. Aaron studied Beth even as he listened to Burt.

When the story concluded with Robert Weeks laughing until the noose cut off his airway, Burt pulled a small leatherbound book from behind his back.

"This belonged to my great grandmother," he said, holding it out. On display, but not for the taking. Not yet. "Emily kept a diary detailing everything that happened before, during, and after the arrival of Robert Weeks. I've... shared parts with those who desired to learn more, and I'm not exactly proud of that. A diary is a personal thing, you see, and I would like to see it in the hands of someone who I know will take the proper care of it."

Burt held the diary with a tight grip, as if afraid to relinquish it.

"Did you get many people seeking this story?" asked Bethany.

A small grin lit his face, somehow made sinister by the crackling fire. "Not so many as you'd think. It's an odd story, this one. Seems to pick who hears it. Think of those poor hanged women and that one guy who got crushed to death in the Salem Witch Trials. Salem is known throughout the world, not just locally, and it's become something of a pilgrimage. In good old Slattery, you've got a man who went to his death with the town believing him a monster, and not in the serial killer sense. He displayed some things that night that might make a man question his belief in God, and he powered that dark magic with the souls of children. If you believe the stories, that is. Thing is, nearly no one outside town knows about it. I always thought about it this way. The story, or maybe it's that damnable house, decides who gets let in on the secret and who gets left in the dark."

"Do you believe that?" Bethany asked.

Burt sat a moment, thinking on it. "I'm not sure I understand it well enough to believe or disbelieve, my dear. You hear stories about your grandparents, same way you two will tell stories about me to your young'uns someday." He interrupted himself with a hearty chuckle. "Point is, I didn't know my Great Gramma Emily. She was gone before I was even born, but I learned a lot about her. Fascinating woman. Couldn't learn enough once my Daddy shared these stories with me." He patted the diary. "She wasn't what you'd call hysterical, and she sure as shit wasn't one of those attention seekers. Otherwise, why would she keep all this to herself, only entrusting family with it?" He paused a moment. "One thing I do understand is I don't like the idea of a man one hundred years dead, or even a story, having that type of authority. A sense of control."

Bethany waited. The old man was building to something, and giving him a shove, gentle as it might be, wasn't likely to speed things along. He nodded to himself every few seconds as though his inner dialogue made points worthy of consideration, then opened his mouth to speak again.

"Aaron, I've loved sharing these stories with you, and I hope you've loved hearing them. Truly, I hope they didn't cost you too much sleep. In a way, I'm bequeathin' it to both of you, but something tells me it's Bethany that's supposed to keep charge of this. I do believe Emily would have liked the idea of this book in the hands of a strong woman."

Bethany's jaw dropped as Burt held the diary out, no longer squeezing it in a death-grip. The leather binding felt warm to the touch and made an almost imperceptible swishing noise as it slid off Burt's palm for the last time.

"Thank you," she said, with tears in her eyes, unable to put into words just how much Burt's trust meant to her. She looked to Aaron and her heart stopped, expecting to find his eyes filled with jealousy, anger, or at the least, incomprehension. Instead, a sly grin spread across his face. He'd known what the old man intended to do. Maybe even gave his blessing.

"Don't think twice 'bout it," said Burt.

"But what do I do with it?"

The satisfied smile slipped off Burt's face and he lifted a hand to cover his mouth. "Well now that I'm not sure I'll be much help with. I sold some portions to a newspaper back in the 1960s. Don't remember what was happening at the time—a few missing kids out in the western part of the state, I think—but I hoped blowing the doors off this whole conspiracy might open up some avenues." He paused, leaving a heavy silence. His cheeks reddened before he spoke again. "Maybe part of me wanted this story to get a Salem-like level of attention. The town selectmen at the time never truly shunned me for it, but they always acted less than friendly afterward. Salem learned to lean into the publicity. I think Slattery just wanted to forget it ever happened."

Bethany held up the book. "Did you share all the juiciest parts?"

"I shared what I thought pertinent. Only realized after the fact how much arrogance impacted that decision. I was no better than the assholes who write the history textbooks, picking and choosing what to share, and letting the public form the opinions I set them up to form. So Beth, I'm puttin' this in your hands because you know right from wrong, and whatever you decide to do, I'm bettin' it'll be smarter and more well thought out than anything a foolish old man could dream up."

Speechless, Bethany smiled, then looked at Aaron, who finally piped up. "I think what she means, Pappy, is she won't let you down. We won't let you down."

"Mighty proud of you two, and while I don't pretend to know the future, I think when the time comes, you'll know exactly what to do." A shadow took up residence across his features. "Maybe nothin' for a while 'cause right now, that house don't pose no threat. Just sits there lookin' like a bastard. But don't it just seem like it's waiting and watching? Breathing, almost? Ready to reach out and grab somebody the first time they forget it's got a history of doing just that?" The shadow passed and the old man whispered, "Maybe it's nothing. Maybe I've just been too close to it for too long."

Burt's eyes appeared haunted, still resonant with thoughts too dismal for the little bit of light the fire provided. When he finally spoke, he accompanied it with a smile that didn't reach his eyes.

"Guess I'll leave you two kids be. Can't keep my eyes open quite as late these days." He sighed as he got up. The last two ice cubes clinked together as he disappeared into the darkness of the kitchen. The sound stopped only when it was replaced by the glug of Burt refilling his glass. He didn't add any more ice.

One more drink to keep the unpleasant thoughts away.

Beth finished her story. "Hold on a second, you two." She pushed her chair back and rose with a muffled groan.

"No fucking way," Travis whispered. "She's not—"

I shut him up with a look. What else could it be?

Beth returned with the swift grace of someone retrieving a well-loved item. None of that "where did I put it bullshit". The diary, which she held with a strange mixture of pride and hesitation, must have spent years stored in a special place. Ready to be unveiled, as Burt Stone predicted, when she knew the moment was right.

"Have you read it?" I whispered. It only felt right, like too much noise would spoil such a solemn moment.

"Every word. Many times over."

I stared at the book, not bothering to disguise the naked greed in my eyes. Maybe Travis had the same look. I didn't know. I didn't care. I only saw the potential key to bringing our baby girl home safe.

"Is there more in there than the newspaper got?"

A small smirk climbed the left side of Beth's face and she leaned forward. "The newspaper barely scratched the surface."

CHAPTER FOURTEEN

I'd like to tell you we sat up all night poring over the contents of the diary, that we dove in with such vigor we had to be careful not to shred the pages. Truth be told, I was only a couple teases away from jumping across the table and snatching the book. I think Bethany saw that because her smile faltered and she withdrew the diary. Maybe not a conscious movement, but noticeable nonetheless.

"I think we'd best save this for the morning," she said, pulling her eyes from mine and staring at the table.

I gritted my teeth so hard that everyone in the room must have heard the grinding sound.

"She's missing now!" I pounded my fist on the table, making all the bottles jump. Travis put a hand on my leg, but otherwise made no effort to calm me down. The voice of reason, unable to see any in this situation.

Bethany didn't look up. She bit her lip to keep the wrong words from escaping. I prepared to unleash another tirade.

Then she spoke. "Maybe you gleaned it from my story, but I don't think Burt quite knew what he had in his hands. I won't be so arrogant as to say I do, but one thing I understand he was right about is the story being a living entity. Stories have power. You don't need to be a reader to believe that. This one has more shadowy corners you're asking me to explore, and my answer is yes, I will help you. It would've been foolish, not to mention awful, of me to whip this thing out if I didn't have that intention. But please don't ask me to read from the darkest parts of this story when the only light we have is the moon." Beth raised her eyes and met mine. They pleaded with me. "I think this is the moment Burt felt coming. Not just me revealing the story, but turning it over to the next guardian. That's you, Elsie."

"You're giving it to us?"

"I'm giving it to you. Just not tonight. As I said, this story has evil in it, the kind that walks at night. It also has twists and turns. It benefits from having a guide. If you'll have me, I'll be your guide. If I can, I'll help get your little girl back. April. And when we're done, I'll gladly see this book out of my house. It's demanded more than enough over the years."

Awe mingled with simmering anger to keep any attempt at speech from bubbling to the surface. I felt Travis studying me. He waited for any kind of sign to charge forward. I didn't give one.

"I know it won't be easy, Elsie. Travis. But try and get some sleep. We'll start unpacking Emily's story first thing in the morning."

Bethany retired to bed, diary at her side, while Travis and I found our way to the cozy guest bedroom across the hall. We could protest and stomp our feet like petulant children—a substantial part of me wanted to do just that—but the best move now that Beth's mind was made up was to use the hours before dawn to get some rest.

I changed into my pajamas and checked my phone. The screen lit up with four missed calls, all from the Southbridge Police Department. Only one of the attempts resulted in a message, friendly yet unhelpful.

This is Officer Lyons of the Southbridge Police. I stopped by to check in on you and Travis, noticed you weren't home, devoting all resources, feel free to give us a call, blah blah blah.

I frowned. Robin hadn't passed our whereabouts on. At least we were still at the point where we could *feel free* to give them a call. A couple more missed check-ins and they might not ask so politely. I snuck a glance at Travis, scowling at his phone. They must have tried him, too. When he felt my eyes on him, he put the phone away and turned the frown upside down, but that's all it was.

I kissed him, pulling him in and running my fingers through his hair. It had been days since we felt like husband and wife. Instead, we played the roles of two strangers standing side by side through tragedy. We stumbled blindly, tripping over the hurdles laid in our path, and only tonight gained some glimmer of hope that we were going in the right direction.

Travis' hands moved to my back, tracing up and down my spine, feeling the trail they knew so well and for just a moment, I forgot anything was wrong. I'd heard tales of couples who experienced grief that made love as a way to bring them closer, to say what they couldn't seem to find words for. Only thirty minutes earlier, I would have deemed it bullshit, but Travis was persuasive. My pajamas stayed on for only a minute or two before I let them fall to the floor.

Mindful of Bethany in the other room, I strained to keep my voice down. I felt alive. I wanted to scream from the fucking rooftops as I held Travis close enough that nothing could ever take him away. The sex lasted two minutes or an hour. Who knows? It was frantic yet gentle, urgent and necessary. And when it was over, neither Travis nor I let go of each other. His breath contained hints of the after-dinner ale mixed with a warm familiarity. It smelled like home.

Wetness cascaded down my cheeks and I pulled his head to my shoulder in an attempt to hide what I considered weakness. Only when his face met my bare skin did I realize he was crying too. His chest hitched and his tears ran down my neck. I don't remember how long we stayed like that, and even if I did, I'm not sure I'd write it down. Eventually sleep took one of us, then the other.

"ELSIE!"

Familiar panic jolted through my body as Travis crossed the grotto to rescue me, but there was nothing to save me from, besides murky neck-deep water. He calmed as he got close and we continued our search. It was me that found the wall, and subsequently the hole in the wall. A brief and futile argument ensued where I informed Travis and Josh I would be the one swimming through to the other side.

"Thirty seconds," I promised. Travis' fingertips gently pressed against the sides of my neck. I reveled in his kiss, then took the deepest breath my lungs could handle and dove under the surface. The tunnel squeezed, and though it was ultimately passable, I didn't know if I could turn around if it came to a dead end. I paddled through, expecting the chasm to open up at any moment. A small tinge of fear took root. Had I misjudged and plunged myself into a watery grave?

My nerves flared in panic as my lungs struggled to conserve air. They began to burn as I paddled forward with increased urgency. Were the walls getting closer together? Relief resonated through my body as the water cleared and I raced forward, lungs at maximum capacity. Then my heart sank. The increased visibility didn't come from natural light. Two glowing green orbs floated before me. They cut through the darkness but didn't cast enough illumination to reveal the identity of their owner.

The burning in my lungs increased as hands wrapped around my throat. Fingers dug into my windpipe. My body thirsted for something cool to quench the burning, even though I knew the water promised death. The tight grip allowed no relief. My body threatened to explode, lost beneath the surface, lost in the basement of this godforsaken house. Black spots danced in front of my eyes, mixing with the prevailing darkness in that underwater cavern. As my brain attempted to check out, my last thoughts were of Travis and Josh. There was nothing I could do to warn them, stop them from coming in after me and suffering the same fate. The man—*thing*—that lived in this house would get them too.

It would be awful.

A final reflex, my body spasmed, legs jerked, but rather than slamming into rough-hewn concrete walls, they tangled in a web of blankets. The dream latched on, trying to keep me under its spell while my lungs still refused to draw breath. The sensation of being surrounded by water dissipated in a heartbeat, but still I felt somebody gripping my throat. Not tremors, but real terrors, gripping my throat and squeezing the life from me. Green eyes floated inches from my face.

I was back in Beth Stone's guest room, but someone else was there, too.

Sleep. The word fluttered through my mind. It was unclear whether my attacker spoke or I imagined it.

My body tried to obey, and then the hands let go. My throat throbbed in agony and I couldn't draw in a full breath. My heart pounded and my limbs refused to obey orders. I listened as a struggle took place. Travis wrestled the intruder away and the meaty thwack of blows landing accompanied the snapping of wood and crash of glass. Was Travis alright? Paralyzed by fear, I hyperventilated in the dark, gasping for short, uneven breaths.

CRASH! More glass shattered. It could only be the window. The deadly shards either avoided me by divine providence or burst outward to litter the grass.

"Get him!" I tried to yell, but nothing more than a wheeze came out. Travis jumped through the broken window and vanished into the night, once more tracking down a green-eyed interloper. This one hadn't been content to merely observe.

I greedily sucked in the cool October air blowing in through the broken window and willed my heart to slow to a normal pace. Eventually it did, beating steadily before a noise in the hall sent it racing once more. The bedroom door flew open and I clutched the sheets and clenched my eyes shut, expecting the green-eyed demon had returned to finish the job. Footsteps sounded, muffled against the carpet, and my eyes refused to open. I couldn't muster the energy to defend myself anyway. It was summoning an image of April, lost and scared, that finally did the trick.

My right eyelid opened a sliver, allowing in a touch of moonlight. Just enough to help me identify the source of the footsteps. Travis stood in the doorway with his hands on his hips, winded and outrun again. He wore only boxers and superficial cuts ran the length of his legs. My body dragged, but the fact that we were both alive gave me the energy to sit up, slumped against the pillows.

He shook his head before I could ask any of the million questions racing through my mind. I needed a faster husband.

CHAPTER FIFTEEN

Travis filled me in on the chase, although there wasn't much to add to the account. He lost track of the person when they darted across the street and into a patch of woods. They wore a robe exactly like the figure we'd spotted at the Weeks House earlier. The green eyes gave us pause, but he still didn't believe it was Weeks incarnate. I dressed as the story withered away to an uncomfortable silence. It lingered for a moment before Travis' eyes went wide and he broke it.

"Bethany!"

He shot up and flew from the room, not bothering to wait for me. A little shaky on my feet, I followed slowly and braced myself against the wall. I knew what I'd find as soon as I stumbled into Beth's room. Travis stood by her bedside, fists clenching and unclenching. He didn't try to perform CPR or frantically search for his phone to call 9-1-1. An initial assessment told him all he needed to know and when I made my way to his side, I saw why.

Whoever tried to strangle me stopped here first, and with no one to pull them off Bethany, they'd succeeded in their ends.

Eggplant-colored bruises bloomed on Bethany's neck and the awkward angle at which her head lay told of the viciousness she encountered in her final moments. I'd never seen a dead body before, save Josh's, and with the walls collapsing around me I had no time to take in the details of his gruesome death. Somewhere in the back of my mind, I knew a dead woman wouldn't look like she was sleeping, but I didn't realize just how different those two images could be.

Bethany didn't appear to be at peace.

"The diary," I whispered, grimacing at how tactless the words sounded resonating in the silence of her tomb.

Travis spun around as if he expected to see it on the nightstand or the dresser. Only then did I notice the disarray of the room. Bethany's bedroom hadn't made the cut for the house tour, but I learned enough about her that day to know she wouldn't keep her quarters in this state. The intruder had pulled drawers from the dresser, flinging clothes across the carpeted floor. How had Travis and I slept through that ruckus? The sheets lay strewn about the floor instead of hiding Beth's body and preserving a semblance of modesty. Travis checked the window but it was locked tight. No entrance through there.

I asked Travis, "Did you come back in through the front door?"

"Yeah," he said. He scratched the back of his head and stared blankly.

"Unlocked?"

He took a moment to answer. "Oh shit."

I shook my head. "I'll never understand why in this community of all places, nobody locks their doors."

"Maybe they will now," said Travis, unable to pull his gaze from Beth's body. "I liked her. A little wacky, sure, but she had a good heart and she wanted to help us. I think she'd have been the first to throw her hands up in celebration when we found April." He waited to see if I wanted to add anything to the impromptu eulogy. Guilt swarmed through me, stealing my words. We brought death to this woman's doorstep and Travis had summed up everything we knew about her in three sentences.

"She's with Aaron now," he continued.

"If you believe such things."

He lowered his head and repeated, "If you believe such things."

"What the fuck do we do?"

He met my eyes for the first time since entering Beth's room and his face held a questioning gaze.

"I don't really see any way we can avoid calling the police."

I nodded, but said nothing.

Not because they can help us, but because that's what people do.

"You've got something in mind," he said. Not a question. "Well, I'm open to it because I've got sore legs from all this goddamn running and my fucking ankles are bleeding. Otherwise, I've got shit else."

"I've got to make a call. I think it'll be a bit before anyone gets here in an official capacity, but I could be wrong. I'm hopeful this mess of a room means they didn't find what they were looking for, and with a little extra time, we will."

"What do you think they were looking for?" He furrowed his brow, and I gave him a look with a generous amount of attitude.

"Oh shit," he covered his mouth in shock. "We killed her."

"Start looking."

CHAPTER SIXTEEN

The phone rang and rang, the digital buzz sounding hollow in the early hours. It was 4:00 a.m. and people who called at such an ungodly hour deserved being sent straight to voicemail. Finally, a sleep-tinged voice came on the line.

"Hello?" it asked from across a sea of dreams.

Hello. Not "Officer Metcalf speaking" or "Southbridge Police Department". She'd actually given us her personal number and probably broken all kinds of regulations in the process. The decision to bring her in seemed a little less desperate all of the sudden and the slightest bit of warmth enveloped me before I remembered the body in the other room.

"Hello?"

I'd become lost in my thoughts. I neglected to think about what to say first, so I blurted anything out to avoid testing her understandably waning patience.

"Robin. Officer Metcalf. Hello." My voice fought its way out of my swollen throat.

A soft creak sounded, maybe the mattress shifting as she sat up. Whispers fluttered far in the background. When her voice returned it had shed any trace of sleepiness. "Yes, who is this?"

"Elsie. Elsie Morland."

"Elsie?" A mixture of shock and stifled outrage. Her voice took on a harsh, whispered tone, as if she didn't want anyone to overhear, although I was fairly positive she was in bed. "You sound strange. What's wrong, Elsie?"

"It's been a night." I bit my lip. She would need to know our actual whereabouts sooner rather than later, but I wasn't ready to go there yet. I changed the subject. "I got a message from another officer. Lyons, I think. He sounded friendly enough, but the underlying tone said he wanted to know why Travis and I weren't at home."

"I'd like to know the same."

"I told you we were at Travis' parents' house."

"In Connecticut?"

"Yes." My stomach clenched. Something was wrong.

"Anita and Daniel Morland, ages sixty-eight and seventy-one respectively. Residents of Ocala, Florida, for the last four years. Those parents?"

"Shit," I said, though that didn't quite cover it.

"Elsie, where are you? And don't say Florida."

I chose silence.

Robin sighed, then continued. "Some people blame the parents when a child disappears without looking at the first piece of evidence, but the prevailing notion was that you and your husband were the victims of a targeted kidnapping. That's how we were proceeding with the investigation, until this."

"We've only been gone a day."

"You can drive to Canada in less than half that time. Mexico with a few more hours."

"Jesus, we didn't think of that." I paused, a light bulb casting illumination on something shoved in the far recesses of my mind. "Why… why are you telling me all this?"

Metcalf didn't answer right away, and when she did, her voice had lost some of its grit. "Because I don't believe you had anything to do with April's disappearance. But," she added, allowing some stern authority to creep back in, "the lying complicates things. I also believe you know more than you told me."

"Why's that?" I swear I almost gulped before I said it, the trademark sign of a guilty person. At least in cartoons.

"It was the part about the green eyes. April said they were glowing and all she could see beyond a sheet of mist. Most parents would look confused, maybe even relieved at thinking their kid saw something easily explainable. Car lights that caught a strange tint or something like that. The blood drained from your faces, you and Travis. If you'll forgive a cliché, you looked as if you'd seen a ghost."

Oh, Robin, you know not what you speak.

"You're not far off."

"Is that where you two are? Trying to chase down a lead on your own? Dammit, Elsie, do you know how dangerous, not to mention stupid, that is? You should have called days ago, or better yet, just told me what you knew before April went missing! Are you trying to get her killed?"

I heard her breathing on the other end of the line, but that was it. I imagined her hand clapped over her mouth, surprised at herself. Two paths existed here. On the one, we could shout our suspicions about Robert Weeks creeping back into existence to steal our most precious jewel. This path would likely see an upstanding couple mocked as conspiracy theorists at best, heretics at worst, and even if one person on the force believed us, I suspect Weeks still would have found a way to get to her.

We chose path two, and now a woman had died. No matter which way we ducked and dodged, we were destined for pain, for misery. I don't know what Metcalf took my silence to mean, but she didn't interrupt. She'd tossed the ball into my court and I held it like I didn't even know what it was.

"I deserved that," I said.

"No, I'm so sorry. That was unprofessional. It was—"

"No, Robin, you're right. The thing is... Travis and I are in over our heads. We were before we even met you. Just didn't know it yet. Calling you for help is the most unfair thing I could've done, because I believe you're a good person, and you'll do it."

A pause. "If I can."

I let out a deep sigh before diving into the deep end. "We're in a town called Slattery Falls."

"Slattery Falls," she repeated. "I've never heard of it, but I'm sure I could find it. What's it near?"

I told her the route and the surrounding towns, feeling suddenly better about bringing her in. When this town didn't reveal itself to a person, it seemed almost like a character reference.

I heard the light scratching sounds of pencil on paper and prepared to drop the bombshell. "We're staying in a bed and breakfast owned by a woman who's been murdered."

"Jesus fucking Christ, Elsie. It gets worse and worse. I'm in derelict of duty by not calling backup and sending them to your location right this fucking minute. In fact, you've got about ten seconds to tell me why I shouldn't!"

"I'm not asking you to cover something up. I'm going to call the police here. I just hoped you might be willing to come up and help us navigate the situation. I don't think they'll want us for a crime. It's a pretty clear case of a break-in gone wrong. It's just..." Now it was my turn to drop my volume to conspiratorial whisper. "She's here, Robin. I can feel it. And there's something going on, trying to keep us from getting to her. If you come help us, I promise we won't keep anything else from you, but shit, could we ever use some help right now."

"Why me?"

"She liked you. *Likes* you," I corrected. "And she trusts you. And that's good enough for me."

I heard a deep breath on the other end of the line that I recognized as forthcoming regret. "About an hour away would you say? Slattery Falls?"

"Maybe less."

"I'll be there as soon as I can. Don't do or touch anything until I get there." A moment passed, but I could still hear her breathing on the line. "Elsie?"

"Yes."

"No more lies. Not even one. I can't help you if I can't trust you."

"I can do that," I whispered.

I gave her the address of Bethany Stone's cottage and thanked her profusely, trying not to overdo it. After I hung up the phone, I stood in the darkness, trying to come to terms with any way we could possibly get out of this unscathed. My mind needed more than sleep to solve a complex puzzle like that, so it wasn't much of an interruption when Travis yelled from the other room.

My ears perked up and my heart thumped at the sound of his voice. I couldn't hear him clearly, but it sure as hell sounded like, "I've got it."

CHAPTER SEVENTEEN

I dashed into the next room and my sore body screamed at the bad decision. Travis held a small book, only slightly larger than the iPhone in my hand. Ancient brown leather graced the cover and a thick strap kept it from falling open and spilling its time-yellowed pages.

"Are you sure that's the right one? Did you look?"

"All due respect to the dead," said Travis, but how many old diaries do you think Bethany kept buried in her underwear drawer?"

I gave him a blank look. "That's where she hid it?"

"I said to myself, Travis, think like a woman. Where would a woman hide something she didn't want anybody to find, even by accident."

"That's more thinking like a man trying to think like a woman, but I can't argue with the results."

He turned his attention to the diary. "Should we open it?"

I started to answer no, but caught my tongue. Instead, I told him about the phone call with Robin.

"Is it good that we're on a first-name basis with her now?"

"Technically we were before we left. I'm just glad she didn't revoke the privilege." I sighed. "She agreed to help, so that can't be all bad." I glanced at the time on my phone. "If she's left already, it can't be more than a few minutes ago and our only instructions are to not touch anything..." I let the thought trail off. "Uh, you didn't make a bigger mess of the bedroom, did you?"

Travis shook his head. "First hunch panned out."

I glanced over his shoulder. We hadn't thought to cover Bethany at first, and though it seemed the respectful thing to do, actually fucking listening to instructions might improve the tenuous grip on Robin's assistance. Without a word, I took Travis' hand and led him to the living room where we sat together on the loveseat.

"I—" My eyes landed on the end table next to Bethany's recliner and I found my words cut off. The book we'd seen her reading earlier, *Mucho Mojo,* rested next to the lamp. Tears welled in the corner of my eyes knowing she'd never learn how the story ended. Such a small thing. Such a small stupid thing, and it brought any momentum to a crashing halt as the tears fell. I knew goddamn well they weren't about the book, but that didn't stop the flow.

Travis let it go for a moment, resting his hand between my shoulder blades and using his thumb to rub in a gentle circle, something I don't think I'd ever mentioned I found comforting.

I picked up the book with a trembling hand. My breath hitched in my chest and my heart stopped as I saw what Bethany had used to hold her place.

"Holy shit," whispered Travis, laying eyes on the little straw doll, bound together into a vaguely humanoid figure.

I shook my head, unable to summon the words.

"You don't think…" Travis left the end of the sentence hanging.

"That Bethany kidnapped April? No. God no," I said with a grimace. I removed it from the book, forever losing Beth's place in the story.

"It looks exactly the same as the one we found outside April's window."

"Remember what I told you in the car?" I asked. "They found another one in Southbridge. Robin wouldn't tell me where, but the guy who had it kept saying 'Weeks'. Over and over."

I turned the doll over, its rough edges scratching against my skin. Simple in its construction, it used the same red twine as the one at the crime scene. I placed the doll on the seat next to me, no longer liking the feel of it on my skin.

"What's it doing here?" he asked.

"There's gotta be some sort of explanation. Maybe just a weird coincidence. I can't believe that Beth…"

"You don't believe in coincidence. And, it's not like we can ask her." Travis studied the cover of Emily Stone's diary, as though willing it to give up its secrets. "Maybe it's in here. We don't have to read it tonight, or this morning, or whatever it is right now."

I shook my head almost violently, willing the words to come. "We don't know what's going to happen once Robin gets here. This might be the only chance we have." I snatched the doll off the couch and shoved it in my pocket. I had no idea what we might need it for, but Travis saw right through me. I didn't believe in coincidence.

He undid the leather strap that held the book closed. One hand worked the journal open, as he kept the other on my back. The paper inside carried the smell of a library—worn, well-loved pages turned again and again. It presented all the heady aromas of time but crammed into a small package. At a glance, the book must have contained nearly two hundred pages, covered in a tightly packed, but neat, scrawl on both sides of the page. Travis skimmed as I leaned over his shoulder. The number of times

I'd read through these pages allowed me to pick up on any differences, though there were few. The diary began as a record of Emily Stone's day-to-day, then about two weeks into those first entries, construction on the house began.

A few additional entries bordered the ones I knew well, but didn't stand out as meaningful—her children's development, neighborhood gossip, and a brief but concerning drought. Possibly these entries were omitted, not by Burt Stone, but by the outlets which published them as not intriguing enough to be newsworthy.

My heart slowly sank with every turn of the page. All the entries seemed the same. Page after page detailing the construction of the house, the odd experiences with the workers, and the first appearances of Robert Weeks in town. My mind demanded new knowledge, and the excitement of holding this original document in my hand quickly died as I read the same chilling, yet familiar, passages again.

The children disappeared, the town mourned and pointed fingers. Tensions rose and eventually the citizens raised torches together and marched on the Weeks House, hanging its residents and lamenting the devastating loss of life they found in the house's basement. I thumbed through the next few pages, trying not to hold my disappointment against Emily. It had been Bethany and her stories passed on from Burt that built up my hope, though it seemed in poor taste to be frustrated with Beth when her body lay cooling in the next room.

"Motherfucker! It's all the goddamn same."

Travis shook his head. The corners of his mouth drooped, echoing my reaction, only a little more quietly.

During the page-flipping frenzy, the diary landed on my lap. I continued the search, only half paying attention when a series of blank pages caught my eye.

"Fucking great," I muttered. "When Burt said he omitted some things, I guess he meant superfluous words. Jesus fuck, Travis, this was our best hope! Our only hope!"

He stared at his lap. More silence.

"And even this last fucking part. More disappointment. A handful of pages left and they're blank. They're. All. Fuck. Ing—" I emphasized every furious syllable with a flip of the page, probably lucky not to tear the brittle paper from its binding. As the last word formed on the tip of my tongue—*blank*—the next page revealed itself to be every bit the opposite.

Before I could shut off my anger and rewire my thought process, two sharp knocks broke the stunned silence.

CHAPTER EIGHTEEN

"You hide the journal and I'll get the door," I whispered.

"Back in the underwear drawer?"

"Okay, I'll hide the journal and you get the door. Walk slow. Give me a head start."

Where to put it, though? I couldn't chance the police finding it among our bags. A woman had been murdered just across the hall from our bedroom, and we were the only other people in the house. Even if we weren't automatic suspects, they wouldn't discount our presence. They'd surely toss the house, so we couldn't hide the book anywhere inside. Panic mounted as Travis' footsteps approached the front door. A trail of broken glass in our room led to the window. Could I sneak out and hide it in the car without drawing Robin's attention? Would it matter?

The waves of anxiety crescendoed toward a terrifying peak and then calmed as realization dawned on me. I promised Robin no more lies. One way or another, she'd need to know about the book. I shoved it down the back of my waistband, then stepped into the living room where I stood in shadow as Travis opened the door. Dimly backlit by the pinkish-purple hue of the rising sun stood Officer Metcalf. She sported jeans and a gray hooded sweatshirt, much to my surprise. I suppose I always thought of police officers like teachers, not having a life outside their line of duty. Then again, she wasn't here in an official capacity. She wore no makeup, but her high cheekbones made the look work for her.

Travis waited in the doorway, silently appraising the woman before him.

"Can I come in?" she asked, not smiling. Her right hand rested on her hip, inches from her unclipped holster.

"Please," I said, unable to stop staring at her gun. "Robin. Officer Metcalf. She's, uh, she's in the bedroom. Beth. Her name is Beth."

"Show me." Robin took her hand away from the holster but didn't secure it. Not yet. She produced a pair of latex gloves from her pocket and slipped them on. "I want you two with me. I'll be quick, but you're not leaving my sight. We've already waited a long time to call the authorities and it's probably not wise to put it off much longer."

I pointed in the direction of Beth's room and Robin strode down the hallway, trusting us to follow her. "Right bedroom or left?" she asked.

"Left," I said. Travis and I exchanged a look then entered behind her. I couldn't stomach another look at Bethany's desecrated body, so I faced the wall as Robin set to work. Travis copied my lead. A small metallic click sounded; the snap on her holster, maybe.

"Sometimes these podunk little towns will have their own ME look, and they'll be able to narrow time of death down to a calendar day," said Robin, "but if we lie and she winds up on the table of someone who actually knows what they're doing, we'd be screwed."

I almost turned around, but the snap of the holster sprang to mind. We'd earned some trust back and sudden movements seemed like a bad idea. I wanted to see through Robin's eyes. I'd never understood the appeal of the forensic, evidence-based, hero-behind-a-badge type shows. Would she uncover something to tell us who broke into the house or would the room be wiped clean?

"We found her a little before four a.m.," I said.

"Okay, any idea how long before that she died?"

"Can't be sure, but not long."

"They'll ask how you know," said Robin. The soft whoosh of moving blankets filled the silence that followed.

I looked at Travis. He raised his eyebrows and mouthed, *tell her.*

"They came for us next," I said.

The shuffling coming from behind us stopped as if someone had flicked a switch. It hadn't seemed that loud until the sudden silence of the house made me miss it.

"You didn't tell me that over the phone," she said. The businesslike tone of Officer Metcalf's voice faded away, replaced by Robin, like the bird. The woman who scuttled like a crab to get a scared five-year-old to open up.

I turned around, expecting that familiar hot flood of tears to bunch up at the corners of my eyes, remembering that terrible dream, waking up and still seeing those horrible, glowing green eyes, being absolutely sure this was my final moment. Maybe the tears were dried up or overworked, but they stayed put.

"I'd have gotten there eventually." I tried to smile at her, embarrassed but genuine. Robin looked me over from head to toe. She put a hand over her mouth, barely muffling a gasp when her eyes reached my neck. The pain pulsated there, but I told myself there hadn't been time for a proper inspection. That I didn't want to see what they'd done to me was probably closer to the truth.

I held out my hands as if to say *ta-da!* then lowered them, unsure what kind of nervous energy made me act so strangely.

"Did you see who did it?" Robin said. "Did you recognize them?"

"That's really hard to explain," Travis chimed in. "There were… details about him that were familiar."

Robin let out an exasperated sigh and put a hand on her hip. Her eyes squinted as she pointed a gloved finger at Travis and me. "Are you going to make me ask you a thousand questions to get one simple answer, or are you gonna start acting like me coming here in the middle of the night to help clean up this fucking mess means something?"

I opened my mouth to speak, then closed it.

"Ah," said Robin. "Okay, so you know exactly why Ms. Stone is dead, and why they came for you, but you can't tell me. Correct?"

"On the contrary, I can tell you." A nervous laugh escaped. "It might take a while, but I can tell you. They won't understand. You might not either, but I promise what I tell you will be the truth."

I didn't think she'd accept that, but she nodded. "Okay, listen up, Elsie. And you too, Travis." She snapped her fingers, a weak sound with the gloves on. "Are you listening?"

"Yes," we said in unison, like reciting a Catholic mass.

"This is the first place we deviate from the truth. You don't know, but you *suspect* the intruder attacked you on purpose. Base your answer on the intensity. Strangling is a personal attack, not usually quick. A robber trying to subdue an unexpected threat will opt for brute force and a quicker route to unconsciousness. You don't know what they could have been looking for. Is there anything else I should know?"

"We checked in under the last name Costa," added Travis.

I expected Robin to be frustrated or even angry, but she laughed, a high, melodious sound not unlike a songbird. "Let me guess. You didn't want the police hot on your trail?"

My cheeks burned. When she put it like that, it sounded pretty dumb.

"Don't be embarrassed," she said, reading my face. "Most people are much worse at hiding from the police in practice than in their own minds. Changing your last name isn't the worst idea, but using your maiden name? Come on, Elsie. Besides, if we'd needed to find you, like really needed to, we could have applied for a warrant to track your phones."

Travis held his phone up as though he'd never seen it before, then shoved it down in his pocket to shield it from receiving a signal. "Yeah, dumbass," he said, playfully. So I punched him. Playfully.

"The name thing is an easy one," said Robin. "You gave a different last name because your daughter has been in the news and you wanted to get away anonymously for a few days."

"Damn, that's smart," said Travis.

"I try. One more problem, and this is the one we really have to sell."

"You," I guessed.

"Me," she confirmed. "They say if you need to lie, put as much truth as you can in there, so that's what we're going to do. Tell the truth. Or at least most of it."

"Think that'll work?" Travis asked.

Robin shrugged and put her hands in her pockets. "If it's more truth than lie, it's easier to keep it straight if we get caught."

CHAPTER NINETEEN

Robin dialed the Slattery Falls Police herself. Either she didn't trust our acting skills or she wanted to relieve a little of the burden. I chose to believe the latter.

After all the build-up, all the anxiety, what followed was somewhat anticlimactic. The local police arrived as the sun peeked over the horizon. They weren't accustomed to murders and a few wide-eyed younger officers patrolled the area, taking in what probably amounted to their first crime scene. They didn't seem particularly interested in me or Travis.

When Chief Hempel arrived—a rail-thin post of a man who appeared more beguiled than competent—Robin switched on her Officer Metcalf persona. From that point, she took care of most of our legwork. She'd stationed us on the loveseat under a warm blanket, insisting we look properly distraught. It wasn't hard to follow that script. We knew to avoid answering as much as possible, but to be short and concise when necessary.

"It's always wise to have an attorney present. Always. But a nice young couple who nearly gets murdered in their sleep doesn't ask for a lawyer when the police show up," she'd told us once they were on their way. "Instead, pretend I'm your lawyer. Dodge and weave until I can be by your side."

Anticlimactic, like I said, because with Officer Metcalf explaining her presence away in the first thirty seconds, the police mostly left us alone and turned their attention to bigger concerns. A young couple has their daughter kidnapped and tries to get away for a few days, anonymously. When an intruder breaks into the house, murders the owner and attempts to do the same to the guests, they panic and call an officer they've grown to trust. An understandable move. I ran the scenario through my head as Robin explained it, and after the third or fourth time even I couldn't separate truth from fiction.

Hours passed and the sun moved west, not quite overhead but nearing that direction. The SFPD gave the house a thorough examination. They even rifled through our bags for clues we might have forgotten to share. The lump of the diary jutted into my back, and what seemed like a miserable hiding place at the time, certainly looked better now by comparison. Especially after they searched our car. A red-headed EMT, barely out of his teenage years and with the acne scars to prove it, inspected the bruises around my throat and the bleeding on Travis' legs. He decided neither warranted a trip to the hospital. My raspy smoker's voice begged to differ, but I didn't fight it.

Officer Metcalf and Chief Hempel reached an accord. Metcalf agreed the possibility of the kidnapping and the break-in could very well be related, and she would act as an intermediary between departments. A scrawny young officer took down our details, returned our belongings, and declared us free to go. That's right, we didn't have to go home but we couldn't stay here. It was a crime scene after all.

An ambulance crawled down Fox Street as we exited the house, lights on, but otherwise silent. A lump formed in my throat as I thought of the paramedics escorting Beth's body to the morgue. As far as we knew, the poor woman had no family to claim her. Guilt settled over me once more, but the thought of April and the extra pages in the diary kept it from overwhelming me.

We relocated to our car and mumbled thanks to the responding officers. The act of looking disheveled and miserable came naturally, barely touching the range of such talented thespians as ourselves. As we looked on, some officers dispersed while others taped off the area. The remaining few stayed just inside the house, making an earnest attempt to look busy.

Robin approached the car and knelt beside it. "Let's get you home," she said, just above a whisper.

I shook my head, slowly and almost absently at first, then with more and more fervor as I warmed up my voice. "We can't. Not yet."

Robin grimaced, the face of someone trying to talk a child out of a bad decision, but with the patience of allowing them a say. "I know you feel like you have to search for April here, but you can't do it indefinitely, and I can't stay with you. Add to that the fact you don't have anywhere to stay."

"It doesn't matter. We'll find somewhere," said Travis, still wrapped in the blanket. Robin gave him a look that said *Oh shit, not you, too.*

"I've heard your story through and I agree there's some messed-up things. I won't even disagree that somebody's gunning for you. In fact, that's probably the best reason to get the hell out of here. But—"

"You haven't heard the whole story yet," I said. "We haven't even talked about Weeks."

I saw anger flare up in her eyes, though she managed to keep it off the rest of her face. "We didn't lie to you," I said, anticipating her next words.

"Well, maybe about the Weeks thing. It's just a long story and we didn't have as much time as we needed."

Robin pinched the bridge of her nose and sighed. "Okay, it's still early and I have the day off. Fucking hell, I've humored you this far, what's a few more hours? But, I'm going to need some breakfast or lunch or whatever. Know any good places to eat around here?"

I smirked. "Not a single one, but if such a place exists, I know exactly where to find it."

We weren't done with Slattery Falls. Not yet.

PART TWO

Apparition Eyes

CHAPTER TWENTY

Main Street offered an embarrassment of riches when it came to choosing a restaurant. The mingling aromas of Italian food, hot sandwiches, and the Slattery Falls House of Pizza, among others, should have combined in a dissonant manner, but after the night we had, almost anything sounded appetizing. You name the type of food, and this stretch of road contained a quaint storefront with booths and a handful of servers to put it on a plate and plop it down in front of you with a smile.

Robin chose a cozy Tex-Mex restaurant called Pastorella's, the kind one can only find in the northeast. Adding to the clearly Italian surname on the sign, the walls popped with decorations that reflected the gringo notion of Mexican culture—trumpets, sombreros, and the kind of poncho Clint Eastwood might wear. Not what I would have gone with, but beggars and choosers and all that. We ordered drinks, and although the mood called for something with a high proof, the hour did not. Frankly, we considered ourselves lucky they were even open for lunch. With drink orders placed, Robin looked back and forth between Travis and me expectantly. I reached back and plucked the diary from my waistband, its newfound home. The book sent a small tremor through the water glasses as I dropped it in the center of the table.

Robin glared at the battered old diary in front of her, unimpressed. She raised her eyes from it to meet mine and awaited an explanation. The waiter had retreated into the kitchen and the dining area was deserted except for us, but I kept my voice down anyway. "Ideally, you'd have time to read the whole thing, but it's lengthy, so we'll give you the Cliff Notes version."

Travis and I spent the next twenty minutes volleying the story back and forth at a near-frantic pace, pausing only when the waiter brought out drinks and collected food orders. If our server thought the awkward silence that greeted him each time he arrived at the table odd, he didn't show it. I'd like to think I didn't look as much like the insane mama bear pedaling conspiracy theories as I felt, but I also didn't really care. I just wanted my cub back.

Recounting the contents of the diary led to sharing the modern-day version of events. Travis wrote them down years ago—for posterity, he said, though I'm not sure even he knew what he meant by that—but that memoir remained tucked away back in our Southbridge home.

Robin listened patiently. She didn't run screaming from the booth or call for backup. Instead, she nodded in all the right places, looked properly horrified as we told her about the events in the basement of the Weeks House, and visibly choked up at the conclusion of Josh's role in the story.

My eyes stung and my voice grew thick as I pushed through that part. Maybe that's what brought her around.

When we finished the story, the three of us sat and stared at our untouched plates. The restaurant was quiet except for the instrumental mariachi band music trickling out of the hidden speakers. Did they always keep it this low or did the waiter suspect this conversation called for a slightly more solemn atmosphere?

"The green eyes…" Robin let the words hang, but the meaning was clear. Not the ones on that decrepit basement-dwelling deer-creature from our story, not necessarily the ones on Weeks himself. No, the ones outside April's window.

"The man at the window," I said. "Yeah, that was the extent of the suspicion until you mentioned Weeks. I hope you understand why I didn't think I could lay that all on you at the time. It would've sounded crazy."

"Still kind of does," said Robin with no humor in her voice.

"Well, we're sorry it took us so long to be upfront, and sorry we gave you the slip."

Robin chuckled, although it never reached her eyes, reminding me that we had done no such thing.

"But there's more," Robin said. Not a question.

I cocked my head. "The murderer?"

"You wouldn't have called me if you didn't see some reason to believe it was related to you two, to April, to that book. Suspicion and coincidence doesn't quite cover it. If it wasn't this Weeks guy, who was it?"

Dropping my gaze, I came so close to prefacing what I said next with some variation on "I hope you don't think I'm crazy", but shit, we had passed that exit some time ago. It wasn't even in the rearview mirror anymore. "The person who attacked me, we saw them earlier that day at the ruins of the house. Both times they had green eyes. Fucking green glowing eyes. Swirling around like the sea during a hurricane and lighting up the whole room."

She didn't say a word, but looked up to Travis with doubt etched across her face. "It's true," he said.

"I didn't imagine it," I said, a touch defensively.

"I don't think that," said Robin, in a tone that sounded like that was exactly what she thought. "You almost died, Elsie. I only wanted somebody who wasn't gasping for air to corroborate."

The sting remained, but I buried it.

"So, it's been twenty-four hours since your arrival," she said. "Do you have anything else to go on?"

"Maybe," Travis said, patting the diary. It sat unopened on the table, inanimate yet somehow threatening. I inched my hand toward it, afraid the additional pages wouldn't reveal anything new, wouldn't get us any closer to our baby girl. I feared the opposite almost as much. I ran my fingers over the soft leather. Robin watched with narrowed eyes. When I slid a finger under the cover to open Emily Stone's diary, her hand landed on the cover, stopping my progress in its tracks.

"What the hell?" I whispered through gritted teeth. She didn't answer, but flicked her eyes toward the back of the restaurant. Less subtle, I turned my head and caught the disappearing heads of the staff dropping below the small circular window that led to the kitchen.

I withdrew my hand. "Probably best to go somewhere else."

"Like where?" asked Travis. "Can't exactly go back to the bed and breakfast."

"I've got a place in mind," said Robin, with a wry grin climbing one side of her face. "I hear it's pretty deserted."

"You've got to be shitting me," said Travis.

"It's not the worst idea," I said, barely able to believe the words coming out of my mouth. I locked eyes with Robin. She was trying to move this investigation along. Maybe that could work to our benefit.

"And," said Robin, "if someone did show up, it might pay to have an officer of the law this time around to assist with the questioning process."

"That officer might be able to run a little faster than the last guy that tried to go after them," I said, holding her gaze.

"I didn't see you running," said Travis, conjuring his most loving fuck-you tone.

Robin and I laughed for a moment before the notion of where we were going returned and a heaviness settled over the table.

CHAPTER TWENTY-ONE

We piled a small stack of bills on the table. Avoiding further interactions with the spying staff seemed like a good idea, lest we spot any green-eyed employees. The image of the woman in town flitted to mind, going about her business before her demeanor changed suddenly and her eyes with it. The kitchen's glass porthole remained vacant. Possessed or not, the staff probably didn't want any more to do with us either. We overpaid, but fuck it. Life is short and it felt like with Robin's help, and the potential hope dwelling in those extra pages, we could put an end to it all that day.

Our two cars climbed the slight incline, once more in broad daylight, and civilization disappeared behind us. Having traversed the route prior, we led with Robin close behind. When we arrived at the taped-off stretch of road, we pulled to the shoulder and got out of the car.

Once again, the shadow of the house loomed over us, in spirit if not physically. Imagine seeing that eyesore taint the skyline every day as a resident of Slattery Falls, and then it just vanishes one day. Maybe the townspeople felt relieved, but you can't create or destroy evil. It simply exists, and if it abandons one form, it takes another. Maybe it scatters to the sky or seeps into the ground or gets sucked into another dimension. Maybe it hitches a ride and heads west. It doesn't die, though.

I shook my head as Robin's car coasted to a stop behind ours. Where had those heady thoughts come from? Jesus, I needed sleep. Preferably without some goddamn lunatic interrupting to choke me into oblivion.

The sharp crunch of gravel under Robin's feet pulled me back into the moment. She ducked under the tape and started up the hill, as if to say "ready or not, here we come". I puzzled at her confident stride. She'd never been here before, yet intuited the right direction. I considered shouting ahead about the cursed doorknob, but an inner voice told me to watch nature unfold for the next few minutes. Travis glanced my way. He appeared as confused as me, but he shrugged it off and we followed our new fearless leader.

Robin skirted around the collapsed façade of the house, past where the ruined books lay scattered among the detritus, and finally settled in the wide-open backyard. A brief cloud crossed her face, like she didn't quite know how she'd gotten to this point, but then she settled down in an unmarred patch of grass, free from the brick-and-mortar refuse.

Travis and I joined her, completing a small circle and ready to begin what felt more and more like a ritual. I pulled the diary free from my waistband and thumbed through it, absently searching for the bevy of blank pages to signify the end of one section and beginning of a whole new one.

The handwriting on the first new page lacked the tidiness of the other pages. These pages held an urgency. I looked at Travis, looked at Robin.

"Ready or not, here we come."

Weeks disappeared months ago, read the undated entry, and my son, Nathan, vanished soon after. No explanation to date, just an assurance that the horrid man's influence is not done with us. My heart still aches for my dear boy, but I must go on. If only for my remaining cherubs, Anthony and Eliza. Of course, the town holds no consensus that the loss of Nathan relates to the hanging or the other disappearances, but sometimes putting on our blinders is what suits us best. I do not believe that Horatio Clark, Peter Alderman, or any of the other elders who pretend their houses are in order, put stock in the words they lay at the feet of the townspeople. They simply want this dreadful business over and done with.

But I've seen the beasts that walk the roads at midnight. Mayhaps they're searching for more children to feed the great underbelly of Slattery Falls. It's possible these are scouts on a mission for their demonic master. I can speculate with great fervor, but I fear approaching them. I fear even sharing my suspicions with anyone but paper and pencil, for I know members of the community who would deem me unfit. A grief-torn mother who lost her son amid a sea of vanished children and can no longer cope with the world at large.

My mind weighs heavy with grief, that much is true, but I trust my eyes more than I trust anyone else in this godforsaken place. The creatures that walk the night travel on two legs, the same as any man. They vary in stature and breadth, leading me to concede there must be more than one, possibly many. As for their gender, I cannot say. They wear long dark cloaks to disguise themselves against the night, allowing them to fade into its tangible shadows.

Not such an unbelievable story, but a wise person, someone who truly pays attention, will ask, how do you see them garbed in the darkest shade of black, traveling in the depths of the night?

The answer is simple, if unsettling. Their eyes. While the hooded cloaks conceal their wearers from head to toe, their faces leer from beneath the robe and the eyes glow a sickly emerald shade, one that cannot seem to decide whether it would rather be green or blue, so it lives in purgatory between the two. They pass my window almost nightly, sometimes more than once. On occasion, they are traveling in the direction of the Weeks House, other times, away.

I watch them, huddled on hands and knees and wrapped in a curtain to hide myself, a mirrored image of these nocturnal deviants, and though their horrible glowing eyes never connect with mine directly, I worry they see me all the same. And some night they will come to me. I want to—No, I must find out where they go, but on my own terms.

I read the first entry aloud, wishing I'd brought something to drink from the restaurant. Though my throat felt less sore, my heart thumped and my mouth went dry hearing my own rabbit-scared voice describe Emily Stone's personal experience which reflected ours so closely.

"Christ Almighty, it's a fucking cult," said Travis.

Robin didn't utter a word, but her pallor spoke for her. A deep-down and petty part of me suspected she didn't believe the story about the green eyes when it came from my lips. To have it corroborated by an account from well over a century ago chilled the blood in addition to lending credence.

"Robin," I said, unsure how to continue once I gained her attention. She looked side to side as if making the voice came from me, or possibly to assure her wandering mind that no green-eyed minions had snuck out from the surrounding woods. Finally, she looked to the sky, confirming the sun still had a lengthy journey before it reached the horizon. She didn't want to be out here at night any more than us.

"It's fine," she said, clearly picking up on our concern. And that's what scared me the most. She'd stayed in a protector role, to safeguard us from overzealous local police, but also to keep us from our worst impulses. For the first time, Robin Metcalf understood there was something bigger to guard us from than yokel police chiefs. "Is there more?" she asked, her tone wavering.

"Do you want me to keep going?"

"In for a penny, in for a fucking pound," she said. Nobody believed the laugh that accompanied it.

CHAPTER TWENTY-TWO

I can hardly stand it anymore. I've made a terrible mistake bringing the Reverend Manheim into my confidence. Surely if anyone could understand the persistence of evil, it would be a man of God. A widow raising two children and mourning a third should never have to bear such burdens alone. Foolishly, I believed there must be someone else in Slattery Falls who felt hanging that brute of a man did not solve the problem.

The reverend spoke his comforting words but could not hide the worry in his deep brown eyes. He's asked to meet with me several times a week. At my home. He didn't come right out and say it, but his tone was unmistakable. He plans to look in on the children. Perhaps he'll take them away. I could never bear that.

Only my mind screams, what if he's right? What if I am making a mountain of a molehill, or worse yet, what if I've invented these demonic creatures altogether? I don't feel as though I'm losing my grip on what's real, but I suspect that's precisely what a mad woman would say to such an accusation.

As far as I can see, there is only one option. I'll need to draw on untapped talents and put on an act for the reverend, convince him the stress of a difficult day drove me to his doors, but that I see the error of my misgivings now. Then I'll have to find out where those devils go at night, where they come from.

And If I should never be heard from again, let this diary stand as a testament to the evil allowed to rear its ugly head in Slattery Falls without consequence.

A light wind rattled the leaves on the trees. Some clung tightly to the branches, hanging on for dear life. Others fell to the ground, covering the grass. I was thankful for those. They provided an early-warning system against anyone seeking to interrupt the work at hand. Research, we would have called it in the old days.

Travis asked to take over the reading, but raspy voice or not, this was my duty.

I prepared to go out last night and follow any sign of the green-eyed wanderers, but I'm ashamed to say I lost my courage. I even went so far as to place a trembling hand on the doorknob, though I couldn't bring myself to turn it. Collapsing by the window, I waited for the creature's return journey, but either it never came or sleep took me first. It wasn't the only time Anthony and Eliza awoke to find their mother huddled on the bedroom floor instead of safe and comfortable in her bed.

The reverend is due to stop by today. I'll need to tidy up, then perhaps I can get some rest. It would not do for him to find a cluttered house or a cluttered mind.

The visit went as well as could be expected. A suspicious look dwelt behind his eyes as I attempted to hide the bags underneath my own with a smile. The children laughed and played, going about their business as babes will. When he left, the reverend wore a sour frown upon his face.

When night fell, I managed my way outside. I'm not proud of leaving my babies unattended, especially in such times, but what the good reverend doesn't know won't hurt him. Dear reader, whoever you are, you'll be pleased to know that both cherubs were safe in their beds upon my return, having not moved so much as an inch. But this small doll I've retrieved. What is it and why did the reverend seem so interested in it? Will it be missed and will it lead back to me? To us?

Let me explain.

My breath caught in my throat. The bulge in my pocket suddenly felt alive, pulsing against my thigh. I caught Travis' glance, his eyes nearly popping from their sockets. They begged me to read on.

Tired though I was, I refused to pass up the opportunity to get to the bottom of these misdeeds once more. I slipped out the door after the first sighting, quieter than the smallest mouse that ever trod across your path, and followed after the night traveler. I'd thought to don my darkest cloak, not unlike the ones the figures wore, and was thus lost to the night. It's only this morning I worry they might possess some type of sight beyond that of mortal man.

The cold air bit at any exposed skin and wiled its way inside my cloak. I kept close to houses, trees, and then storefronts in an attempt to blend in with my surroundings and become invisible. The green-eyed rogue gave no hint they were aware of my presence, continuing on their way at a clipped pace.

Very suddenly, they came to a stop in front of Rutger's Barber Shop. The storefront stood deserted and the hooded menace waited a moment as though expecting someone to let them in. Then they knelt and busied themselves at the side of the door. Their form shrank and any passerby could have mistaken them for a shadow cast by the moon. Finished with their business, they turned in an about face and retreated, passing by as I attempted to become part of the brick façade I had pressed myself against. If they took notice of me, they gave no sign.

I didn't move for at least two or three minutes and the streets contained no sign of life during that interminable time. I convinced myself that the moment I chose to move, the beast would bear down on me, extinguishing my life as it forced me to stare into those terrible eyes, leaving my babies all alone in this desolate world to fend for themselves. But like following the hooded figure in the first place, I eventually drew up the courage and breathed a sigh of relief when the area remained as barren of life as ever.

There was nothing to see in front of the barber shop at first and I couldn't imagine why they had traveled all this way. Then a light spot against the darker brick caught my eye—a piece of straw wedged into a spot where someone had meticulously scraped the mortar away. I pulled it free and a straw doll, no longer than my hand emerged. It was crudely made, lashed together with red twine and only vaguely resembled a human-like figure. I nearly dismissed it as coincidence. Surely, these monsters did not roam the night to deliver children's playthings. Something about the doll's weight convinced me otherwise. Not the physical weight, you see, though I'm not sure I have the right words to describe my meaning.

Something was wrong with the doll, and the only thing that seemed a worse idea than secreting it away in my cloak and taking it home was to leave it there. I cannot explain the rationale, but these creatures were up to no good and somehow it linked to an innocent child's toy.

I'm writing this in haste as the sky grows a little less dark. I will need sleep before the babies wake, for I'll be at my errands again tomorrow night. I've seen the direction the infestation is heading, yet I know not where it is born.

The reverend arrived this morning with a spring in his step, whistling a melody as he entered the house. He showed no interest in the children but took tea at the kitchen table with me. Something shifted in his eyes when he caught sight of the doll. His demeanor became quite serious and he excused himself with a false smile. As he stood, his trembling hand moved forward to seize the doll, but he quickly snatched the hand away, wincing as if in pain. He offered a hasty apology and made for the door, slamming it behind him.

I don't know what I was thinking, leaving such things about during his visit. My mind would not have made such careless mistakes before. I've hidden the doll here. I won't share where. Gut instinct has steered me correctly so far and I believe I'll trust it once more.

CHAPTER TWENTY-THREE

We skimmed the next few entries. The encounters with Reverend Manheim became more frequent and though he did not mention the doll again, Emily suspected the thought was never far from his mind. Emily had been unable to catch any of the creatures making their return journey, but followed several more under cover of darkness. Each time she feared discovery, but managed to evade detection, and each time she returned home with another straw doll. Besides the nightly forays to retrieve them, she kept her guard up during the day. More than once, her watchful eye stumbled across little straw men throughout town, always hiding from the sun.

If Emily had any theories about why these green-eyed bastards spent nightfall planting talismans—as she began to call them in later entries—around town, she didn't share them. It was hard to nail down the tone of these entries. Increasingly paranoid wouldn't be off the mark, but paranoia usually implies an unknown reasoning. Poor Emily Stone, who I commiserated with long before these new pages fell into my hands, took on a town-wide conspiracy with no one else on her side. And we'd gotten her last remaining relative killed by one of the monsters who perpetrated it.

Fuck us.

Weeks and weeks of collecting the little dolls, I imagine the hoods must know someone has discovered their plan. Do they check back on the locations? Do they understand their talismans have gone missing? I cannot know for sure, and I am probably pressing my luck at this point.

My babies have noticed what all these nightly errands do to me. They say I appear thin and pale. "Mother dear, you look unhealthy", they say. They cannot understand this sacrifice is for them, for their continued safety. Because clearly Robert Weeks reaches out from the grave to take more from a town he has already harmed so much.

I am rambling, I realize, but in a much more real way, I am delaying putting to paper what I first opened this diary to write. After days and days of, well, not failures, but they cannot be classified as successes either, I managed to follow one of the creatures to their origin point. I can't imagine why I was surprised. As we took corner after corner at a rapid pace, I tried to keep the shadowy creature within my line of sight while also attempting to avoid drawing suspicion down on myself. Not an easy feat, I can tell you.

As with their previous forays into town, the creature traveled with a sense of urgency, but made no moves to watch its surroundings. Either they worried not about being caught distributing the straw dolls, or worse, they knew any attempts to stop them stood no chance of success. When the hooded figure exited the town proper, my blood chilled within my veins, every natural sign in my body screaming to turn and go back home. The beast moved in the direction of the deserted Weeks House.

Further into nature, concealing myself became more difficult as I trusted the thick trunks of the forest's oaks to shield me from discovery. The creature's feet pounded against the packed dirt of the path, carrying through the trees with an ungodly ruckus. It allowed me to keep my distance without fear of losing their trail. When they approached the front gates of the looming house, its angles all wrong and its shadows roiling and slithering as if alive, the creature skirted around the rear of the house. The great oak tree from which we'd hung Weeks still stood on the grounds. Two nooses dangled from its scraggly branches—a warning to others to steer clear of this cursed place.

Once around the house, the cloaked figure dashed into the woods, and I believed myself mistaken. The final destination of this monstrous being simply took it within the vicinity of the damned house. I tell you, I did not look forward to entering a thickly wooded area, and even wondered if this hooded beast had indeed tracked me and now lay in wait.

The moon's generous light did nothing to cut through the canopy and I found myself wandering in darkness. Beside myself with worry and trembling with fear, I thought it best to turn back. I almost did, in fact, but a soft glow emanating from a break in the leaves caught my attention. I could still see the treeline and even the menacing silhouette of the Weeks House, and my heart hammered within my breast as I realized the situation I'd gotten myself into. Nothing good lay forward or behind. An impending sense of doom hung over me, no different than the house itself.

Knowing I'd curse myself for a coward if I turned and ran, and not even sure I'd make it out unscathed, I continued forward. I stopped frequently to listen for signs of life, but none existed outside of my own breathing and my racing heart. As I rounded a particularly thick bushel of trees, I came across a sight that had no business in these woods. In any woods.

A staircase descended into the earth. It glowed an unnatural shade of green, not unlike the eyes of the hood, and hummed gently against the silence of the night. The closer I drew, the louder the buzz seemed to grow, almost insectile. How could I have missed it before? It should have terrified me, but rather it enticed me, and I placed one foot upon the stone step and began the descent. What would I do if I ran into one of those creatures on the narrow staircase?

The steps descended into the heart of the hill on which the horrible house rested, going down further than logic should have allowed. I couldn't shake the sensation that I'd entered a living, breathing thing. The walls pulsated with inhales and exhales that resonated more slowly than my own, yet held a steady rhythm. When finally my feet found solid ground, a long tunnel stretched before me. Deserted and desolate, to such a degree I feared I'd lost the path of the treacherous creature. Nevertheless, I pressed forward, my echoing footsteps the only sounds. Did this series of tunnels connect to the house's basement? The place where they found the children? It seemed impossible, but my understanding of that word had altered quite drastically over time.

When the tunnel could stretch no further, it reached a dead end. Only when the lights went out did I question where they came from in the first place. Quickly, they flashed back on and I spun, searching for the source. Though the cavern was illuminated, the light appeared to originate from the air itself and I understood I'd come to the right place. As I became accustomed to the returning light, goose pimples rose upon my skin and I knew this to be a different tunnel. The walls appeared the same and the direction I'd come from still stretched on infinitely, but this location held a warmth the former tunnel lacked, and though peril still floated freely through the air, it lulled me into believing I had gone the right way.

The wall before me opened up just then. It did not disappear or even swing like a door, but it was there and then all of the sudden, it was not. As the tunnel unveiled a new destination, an advent of voices crashed upon my ears, striking terror deep in my heart. The murmurs bounced off the walls, not resembling speech so much as song. I continued forward, though the smooth bare walls offered no protection from potential discovery. I would simply have to trust in the luck that had blessed me thus far.

The voices grew louder as I took each tentative step, carefully designed to make as little noise as humanly possible, and closed the gap. Up ahead, the wall gave way to an immense cavity and an array of lights flickered out into the tunnel. Not just shades of green, though they were certainly present, but hues of pink, purple, and orange as well, almost if the setting sun were contained within whatever room lay ahead.

Arriving at the opening, for I could not consider it a true doorway, I steeled myself and sucked in a deep breath before peering around. I expected to come face-to-face with the creature and have my life stolen from me, yet some force deep within plunged me forth anyway.

My expectations were not met. Far from it, in fact. Anticipating another room formed from stone, my mind took a moment to process what I saw. The floor dipped down an immeasurable amount into a pond of sorts, water sluicing against the edges of the tunnel. As the gentle luminescence emerged from thin air, the colorful lights seemed to stem from the ground itself, distorted by the surrounding water to create an almost hallucinogenic mirage. Within the water were no less than a dozen hooded figures, their backs to me, and their bodies submerged to the shoulders in the still water. A scream rose in my throat, which I managed to stifle at the last conceivable chance, but none of the figures turned to face the slight woman intruding on their ceremony. Their voices, too beautiful for the occasion, harmonized and floated around the room, an auditory version of the ever-changing light.

Enough activity flowed through the room to distract me for hours, but eventually my eyes found the source of their attention. The far wall eschewed the other colors of the spectrum, glowing only that mixture of green and blue where the center of the ocean stores its secrets. As I watched the light undulate and dance across the single wall, they proceeded with the ceremony. One figure sank below the water, their voice lost to the choir. Each passing second where they did not emerge again caused unbearable tension within my chest. Rather than the first participant returning, a second disappeared, then a third, and on and on.

With every disappearance, the sustained tune grew thinner and more discordant, as though the water claimed those with the sweetest voices first. When only one creature remained, it performed an intimate solo for its fallen brethren, then sank beneath the surface to join the numinous dead. The song, eerie to begin with, grew increasingly so as it vanished, leaving me floating in a pregnant silence. I did not understand what I had seen, except to know it was why I had come.

A jolt of fear resonated through my body at the thought that I might be trapped down here. After all, I had experienced some form of unearthly transport, but the terror was short-lived. The underground cavern had caved to my whims, demonstrating its living nature. It guided me safely to this point and it would either see me out or it would keep me prisoner. The lack of control was oddly comforting.

I retraced my steps with no urgency and soon came to the bottom of the staircase. Though it had seemed nearly endless upon my descent, the trip to the surface moved more quickly. The journey home was equally uneventful. Another night passed where the babies did not toss or turn in my absence.

With as many new questions as answers floating around in my mind, I suspected the turmoil to keep sleep at bay. I recall my head coming in contact with my pillow, thoughts racing inside my head, prepared to search for answers internally, but before I could play detective, sleep came and wrapped me in its loving arms.

I managed a few hours of sleep, then woke abruptly to log last night's events before they could escape my mind. As I finalize this entry, the children continue to slumber. Out of the kitchen window I can see the Reverend Manheim approaching for our meeting. He is before his time and I must hide these writings before he reaches the door. So silly of me, but from across the street, his eyes appear a subdued shade of green. I always thought them to be brown.

CHAPTER TWENTY-FOUR

I turned the page and found nothing after that entry. Not wanting to repeat my earlier mistake, I flipped through each page, meticulously checking front and back before accepting I had just read Emily Stone's final correspondence.

Had the autumn air grown cooler while I read? How much time had passed and how long did we have until it grew dark?

The last entry contained an odd finality that gave me chills. It left me with so many questions about what happened next and made me fear the worst. I racked my brain for anything in our research I'd ever stumbled upon relating to Emily's fate but came up empty. Could Weeks have possessed the reverend and come for her? Bethany might have been able to shine some light on the rest of Emily's days, but for now that door remained closed.

Moments passed after I shut the diary with a soft thump. I continued staring at the worn cover as though it might reveal one more secret. When I glanced up, Travis and Robin both looked at me expectantly.

"Travis," I said, ignoring Robin for the moment. "Do you think there's any chance the basement is still down there? All of it?"

He shook his head, his response coming a little too quickly. "We saw it collapse, Els. It damn near fell on us." He dropped his gaze, searching for the right words, but Robin found them first.

"I don't understand. What in that story makes you think it's still down there?"

"We've been in that pool," I said, unable to remember just how detailed we'd been during our recollection at the restaurant.

"Grotto," said Travis. "We called it a grotto." He studied me and I couldn't help wondering what exactly he saw in me. An unfamiliar woman teetering on the brink of insanity? A partner in desperate need of assistance?

Whatever he searched for came quickly as his trained eyes suddenly lit up with understanding. "The dreams."

I nodded, sneaking a glance at Robin, who looked perfectly lost. "It's admittedly speculation, guesswork, what have you, but Emily Stone revealed an access point where that cult or whatever the fuck it is can communicate with Weeks."

Robin's puzzled look stayed put. "How do you know they were communicating with Weeks?"

"What else could they be doing? That's his domain." I hated the way the last word sounded, but it felt like the right one.

"And you don't believe they drowned?"

"Not for a second. Cult behavior, sure enough, and I suppose singing while they go to their doom wouldn't be wildly out of character, but there's a hole in the wall down there, underneath the surface, and the first time I went through… things got weird," I said, unable to think of a better way to phrase it. Travis raised an eyebrow.

Robin took the new information in stride, determined not to confirm or deny her belief just yet. She did, however, have some difficulty keeping the *what-have-I-gotten-myself-into?* off her face.

"The way the basement reforms itself," said Travis. "If even a piece of Weeks remained, I don't know that it's out of the realm of possibility for it to happen again." He paused, then after a couple false starts got his meaning across. "I thought the dreams must be trauma. Bad memories invading your sleep, homing in on our second chance. I'm sorry, Els. It was just so easy, once we… once we buried Josh to put all that controlling stuff at the back of my mind. I couldn't stand not being in charge of my own destiny, and the fact that the dreams were anything but dreams. I couldn't wrap my head around it."

The genuine sorrow in his tone said more than an apology ever could. He believed he'd failed me, failed April. But we wouldn't get anywhere wallowing in misery.

I reached for his hand. "You're not alone in that. You've known me for a long time, Travis." I smirked. "Am I really the type to keep quiet when I think you're doing something wrong?"

The atmosphere lightened enough to continue on. "So, combine the living basement with a working knowledge of where the green-eyed murderers come and go from…" I sighed. "It doesn't *not* make sense. Plus, it's kind of all we have to go on."

"So we're looking for a staircase in the woods?" asked Robin, with no trace of mockery in her voice.

"That's about the size of it." I looked up at the sun. "I'd say we have a few hours before dark. Who knows if the hoods can come out before then, but it certainly seems to be when they're most active."

"The hoods?" asked Robin, with a trace of amusement.

I held up the diary. "The word of Emily. Seems fitting. A cult is just a glorified gang, anyway."

"I guess I'd feel better if we had a weapon," said Travis, absently searching the rubble as though a knife or baseball bat might appear. If one magically did, it was probably something we didn't want to lay hands on anyway.

"I've got us covered," said Robin. She patted the holster on the side of her jeans. "Let's just hope there's no need to use it."

We stepped into the woods with a few things in mind. Emily had followed the creature in from the back of the house. That left a pretty big patch to cover, but narrowed down the area a little. Emily also noted that she could see the house from where she first encountered the staircase. The house wasn't exactly small when it stood, but it did mean we weren't looking at a hike that went on for miles.

Crossing the treeline reminded me of the first time we set foot inside the house, like the evil that resided within those walls couldn't be contained within such a small space and sank its claws into the surrounding lands. An eerie calm floated among the trees, gently rustling the leaves in a way that might soothe on any other day. A sound that could cover approaching footsteps.

"Split up?" asked Travis.

"Don't tell me you forgot the rules," I said. "We never split up, jackass."

"Husky means we bail," he said, under his breath.

"Am I interrupting something?" asked Robin.

"Long story," I said. "Before we got pulled into this mountain of bullshit, this dork and my cousin were amateur ghost hunters. Josh had a system, rules and everything. A little bit like the rules for surviving a horror movie, I guess. But one of the big ones was you never split up. Too much can go wrong to possibly justify the little bit that can go right."

"Makes sense," said Robin.

The forest landscape all looked the same. We searched for inconsistencies along the path and any ominous green glowing. No one wants to look for a staircase that leads to a haunted pool in the middle of the night, but at least darkness would allow us to see the glowing green eyes better. I turned every so often to make sure I could still see out to the clearing where the house once stood, keeping it in sight both on Emily's word and so that we didn't end up irretrievably lost in this wooded maze.

"Mommy."

Soft, not much more than a whisper, but the voice was unmistakable.

My stomach dropped and I frantically searched in the direction the voice haled from. Directly in front of us.

"Mommy."

Higher this time. Did it come from the trees? My heart pounded like a bass drum, threatening to drown out another call.

"April? I'm coming, baby!" My voice echoed through the forest, causing Travis and Robin to jump out of their skins.

"Elsie, what the fuck?" whispered Robin. Her owl-wide eyes searched for the cause of my outburst.

Tears welled in my eyes. "You didn't hear that?"

"Hear what?" asked Travis.

"Our baby. You didn't hear her call?" Everyone stood absolutely still. Even the wind took a brief hiatus so that we could clearly hear the silence the forest offered up. We held that position until a breeze returned, rattling the tree branches. Then the tears dropped.

"I'm sorry. I swear I heard—"

"Maybe you did," said Travis, drawing an odd look from Robin. "He knows we're here. Now he's trying to draw us out. Get us to do something stupid. If you hear it again—"

"Her," I said. Now, more than ever, we couldn't let our daughter become past tense. Forgotten. "Hear her."

"Her," he corrected. "If you hear her again, let's see if we can pinpoint where her voice is coming from."

"Okay," I said, feeling the furthest thing from that, but listening as hard as I could.

CHAPTER TWENTY-FIVE

My thoughts raced. They grew so loud and chaotic I became concerned they would drown out April's voice. Why was I the only one who heard her? A trick of the forest's acoustics, maybe, or a trick of a different sort entirely? God, this place had them in spades.

No further calls came as we forged deeper into the woods. The crumbled foundation waited at our backs, growing farther and farther away, but always remaining in sight until one rapid spin brought me face-to-face with nothing but trees. Darkness weaved between each trunk like spiderwebs, making visibility a distant memory

"Travis," I whispered. He stopped in his tracks as though I were warning him of a steep drop-off only inches away. "The entrance to the woods. It's gone."

"Of course it is," he said, more of a frustrated sigh in his voice than fear or anger. He scratched his head and turned to survey the new landscape. "Christ, it all looks the same."

"Why don't we just turn back and regroup," suggested Robin.

"It doesn't work that way. Might actually take us deeper into the woods," said Travis. "The last trip, we saw the whole fucking place turn into a maze, same as Emily described, and I think we might be right back in that same shit situation."

Robin thought for a moment, putting two fingers to the side of her chin. "What did it mean when the house changed itself around?"

Travis furrowed his brows and looked at me, not quite shrugging his shoulders, but the gesture evident on his features.

"Usually meant the house was herding us. *Weeks* was herding us," I added. "One path disappeared to shine light on another. We'd get a choice presented to us but free will was an illusion. If we went a different way than we were supposed to, the structure would rearrange to take us back where it wanted us to go."

"Our fate," said Travis.

We'd never spoken of it in these terms before but as soon as the words left his mouth, I knew they were true.

"So that means we're not meant to get back to the foundation," Robin said. Her voice quivered like *Jurassic Park* Jell-O.

"Yeah, that's probably right," I said. "It also means something is likely to happen soon." I looked around, expecting trees to part like the Red Sea, for the ground to open up, for a fairy tale-esque cottage to materialize and slowly creak its door open. Only ragged rows of trees stared back. The forest grew darker by the minute as the sun's light vanished faster than it should have, plunging us into nighttime.

As the shadows that separated each trunk thickened, my heart thumped out of my chest waiting for a set of glowing green eyes to emerge from the pitch. The sun disappeared, leaving us at the mercy of the moon. The light cut through the canopy, thin from fallen leaves, and though better than nothing, it did little to illuminate the next step of our journey.

I pulled out my phone and turned on the flashlight app. Instead of a bright beam, it let out a weak flickering candlelight. I shook the phone as though it might help. "What the fuck?" I knew, of course I knew. Another one of Weeks' tricks. Spin the walls, jumble the forest, turn down the sun, make flashlights useless. I knew the tricks, but God they made me furious. Especially with April out there in the dark.

Then the noises began.

Somewhere in the woods of Slattery Falls, a thousand occurrences of strained creaking resonated from every direction. The night April disappeared came rushing back—an approaching Nor'easter. It sounded as if the forest had converted roots to legs and set all of its denizens free. With the moon and flashlights equally ineffective, my imagination conjured some real *Wizard of Oz* shit.

Had there been even a hint of wind, I think my desperate mind could have kept my nerves at bay, but the air remained as still as death. The creaking grew so loud I clapped my hands over my ears. It sounded as though the trees had closed in all around us. The cacophony filled our heads with their dying shrieks, screaming the only way a tree knew how.

Travis and Robin joined me. I grabbed for anything familiar. Skin, cloth. It didn't matter so long as I didn't get a handful of bark. At the merest hint of the rough scrape of wood on skin my heart would give out. I found a flesh-and-bone hand, squeezing its warmth with everything I had. It returned my grasp and the cold metal of Travis' ring told me I'd found safe harbor. I opened my eyes as wide as they would go, but the living forest stole the moon's dim glow. Pitch dark bathed us as unknowable nightmares danced in the inky blackness. Was April among their number?

A sweaty grip gently took my free hand. *Robin*. Her hand enfolded mine as the trees' screeches climbed to a deafening level.

Buried within the clamor, I swear I heard April again. *Mommy.* I answered her, but no matter how loud I screamed, the wailing woods drowned out my voice. Thunderous percussive booms joined the symphony, spaced far enough apart that whatever traveled toward us must be massive.

Boom!

Seconds passed, filled with the debilitating orchestral arrangement of hellish noises. Branches cracked and snapped like bones.

Boom!

I dropped to my knees and let go of Travis. Let go of Robin. Leaves swirled around us, scratching at exposed skin as they jetted past.

Boom!

I slammed my hands over my ears again, waiting for the creatures of the dark to close in on us.

Boom!

Then it stopped.

As if someone had flicked a switch. Silence pervaded the forest, broken only by a distant humming sound.

Teeth still gritted, I opened my eyes, almost hoping for the continued darkness so I didn't have to see what could have caused that nightmare to end so abruptly. Only I didn't find darkness. The trees stood as I remembered them, spaced apart and still in the stagnant air. The calm after the storm or the eye of the hurricane?

An eerie green light showed them clearly. My heart thumped and my pulse pounded, expecting to find sinister emerald eyes starting out from the dark. But no, this light came from an object with no earthly business in the center of the woods.

A stone staircase.

And it didn't go up.

CHAPTER TWENTY-SIX

We padded through the grass, approaching the staircase not unlike how one might creep up on a sleeping tiger. A creature beautiful to behold but brimming with danger. I didn't fully trust anything that glowed that shade of green and each crunchy leaf on the forest floor threatened to shatter the calm. Within a few footsteps of the glowing stone, we stopped. The hum grew louder but it soothed, like a white-noise machine designed to ease worries and help bring sleep.

Travis and I leaned in as Robin waited a few steps behind. We peered down the stairs, noting six or seven steps before the rest vanished into a pool of tangible darkness. The shimmering green light escaped from between each stone of the doorway, as though its architect had used radioactive mortar. It provided an ethereal glow on the outside, but cast no shine inside the stairwell.

"Ladies first?" asked Travis, the fucking coward. He followed the question by practically throwing himself over the threshold to take the first step. Smart move. He knew I'd have accepted his offer.

I followed him in and watched the dark pool below remain stalwart as we moved toward it. Travis sank his foot into the murk and a grimace spread across his face. Relief replaced the pained look as his foot met solid ground. Confusion set in when he took another step.

"What the fuck?" he muttered. "It's flat."

"Flat like no more stairs?" I asked.

"I guess. I still can't see my feet," said Travis.

"How's the ground feel?" asked Robin.

"Solid, more or less. Just feels like more stone, but the shadows by my feet. They're moving. Like the dark has a current."

I stepped next to Travis and watched black oblivion swallow everything below my ankle. The murkiness chilled my feet, as if I'd plunged my leg into a creek mid-winter. When I lifted my foot back into view and placed a hand against it, the shoe was bone dry. The icy mist slowed my movements, like something unseen below the surface gripped the soles with every step. It lapped at my ankles, trying to halt my progress. We pushed on, but it was like trying to run uphill with boulders strapped to our legs.

The chill crept halfway up my shins. Was it my imagination or had the shadows climbed since I last checked?

A shiver shot through me as I turned to the stairs, hoping to see moonlight trickling in from above. Even trees would bring comfort. Some connection to the outside world. What I saw instead didn't shock me. The stairs numbered far beyond the six or seven we had traversed. They curved and climbed endlessly before disappearing into the same nebulous dark that surrounded our feet. We had only descended a few feet underground, but the dizzying sight which ascended to the heavens begged to differ.

As I weighed whether or not to bring it to Travis' attention, I heard him whisper, "Fucking Christ." His neck craned upward and his hands were on his hips. "He took our way out."

Robin didn't make a sound, simply gaped. Is it irony when an untrustworthy landscape only serves to build a bridge of trust between you and your virgin compatriot?

When she picked her jaw up from the floor, she managed a few dumbstruck words in the vein of "I don't believe it."

I grabbed her gently by the sleeve and felt her recoil under my touch. "That's our cue to move forward. I'm thinking if we spent our time and energy climbing those stairs, we wouldn't find what we were looking for at the top. Assuming they even ended."

Robin nodded, then froze mid-head bob when a small voice echoed through the… whatever the hell kind of room we were in.

"Mommy." The voice bounced around the darkness that seeped up from the floor and passed for walls. Its desperate sound tore at my heart with every echo. I withheld my answering scream, not wanting to give in to the force that delighted in taunting me. My stomach ached. Not answering, not making every effort to let April know I'd come, made my chest tight. I turned back to Robin, finding her still frozen. Just behind her, Travis stared ahead into the darkness, his forehead wrinkled in concentration.

"You heard it, too," I said.

They simultaneously broke their stupor and, as if on cue, the three of us filled the void with our screams, our pleas. The acoustics turned three voices into six, into twelve, into multitudes, and I clutched onto the hope that April could hear a fraction of the din. I needed her to know someone was coming to get her.

Travis moved in the direction he had heard April's voice. Then he disappeared. Not into the black hole ahead, but down, sucked in so rapidly I might have missed it if my eyes weren't trained directly on him. No time for a scream. He was there, then gone.

Gone.

Against my better judgment I lunged forward, tripping over my own graceless feet. I felt them go out from under me and couldn't stop myself as I came face-to-face with the cold, black muck. Despite its mysterious consistency, I expected to plow through the shadowy barrier and smack my face on the ground. When it rose to greet me, I barreled through like a child performing a cannonball into the pool on a warm summer day.

SMACK.

My body hit hard cement in the center of a brightly lit room. I rolled over and bumped into Travis. He groaned, cradling his right arm.

"Are you okay?" I asked.

"Landed on my back and bashed my shoulder, but I'll live. You?"

"I'll feel it tomorrow." A jolt shot through my heart. Tomorrow.

"Do you know where we are?" he asked.

I looked around. The ceiling we fell from loomed high overhead, farther than one should be able to drop from unscathed. My stomach rolled around, transitioning from dizzying tumble to nauseous fear.

I knew this room.

Shattered wood lay scattered about the floor—remnants of a table and chairs destroyed by nature, or at least a lack of natural boundaries. It looked like a scene from *The Sorcerer's Apprentice*. Mickey Mouse chopping an army of possessed brooms to bits with an ax when they did his bidding a little too well. A shiver ran through my body as I climbed to my feet, shaking off the dull aches and pains from the spill. Travis stood next to me, brushing himself off. I didn't need to ask if he recognized the location. His eyes made that clear.

"Elsie! Travis!"

A dull and muffled voice sounded from some undetectable point in the room. My heart raced, thinking it might be April, but no. *Elsie. Travis. Not Mom.* This voice belonged to an adult.

"Robin?" I called, and a silence lingered before the distorted voice called, "Are you guys okay?"

"Yeah, fine. Come through the floor." Only once it left my mouth did I realize how ludicrous it made me sound.

"Did you say come through the floor?"

"Yeah, like we did."

"It'll be fine," called Travis. We caught each other's eye, both clearly in the midst of a similar thought. *Would it be fine? Would she even end up in the same place as the two of us?*

I frowned and hoped I hadn't just convinced our law officer friend to take a portal into non-existence.

"On three?" called the disembodied voice.

"On three." Travis and I found our way back to the approximate area where we had come through.

"One." Our voices rang in unison with Robin's a little distant and off-center.

"Two." We put our arms out and tensed our muscles, ready to break her fall.

"Three." Clasping hands, we waited for her appearance, and she didn't disappoint. Robin didn't so much drop from the ceiling as beam into existence with a soft green glow about four feet from the floor. Unfortunately, it was four feet off the floor on the opposite side of the room.

She crashed to the ground unceremoniously, narrowly avoiding the detritus strewn about during our last trip to this room. The former dining room/ball room had objected with vigor to its own uncreation. I closed the gap with Travis close behind, but Robin popped to her feet on her own.

"Couldn't have warned me about the crash?"

"Thought you might not make the trip," said Travis, sporting a grin.

"Probably right," said Robin, as she dusted herself off and looked around the enormous room. "What is this place?"

"We were down here last time," I said. "Weeks gave us this big Bond villain monologue, then chased us down to the next floor."

Robin paused her survey of the room to catch my eye. She bit down on her bottom lip and raised her eyebrows. "Should I even ask what was on the next floor?"

I shook my head. "I don't think we're supposed to go that way. The grotto we're trying to get to should be above this room. The other way only leads down and, uh, we don't want that."

"Els, look around. There's no way up or down."

God dammit. He was right. Four very solid walls surrounded us, spread out and spacious, but no less a prison cell. "No, it's okay, because we know how this works now. A doorway will open when we need it."

"Or it needs us."

Bending our don't-split-up rule, we spread out, searching every well-lit crevice in the room in an attempt to find our way out. As much as I hate to admit it, I would have welcomed Weeks' booming baritone as an alternative to treading water.

In a room filled with splintered wood, a blackened item among the rubble caught my eye. I knelt to inspect the piece of fabric, run it through my hands, forgetting my don't-touch-potentially-cursed-shit rule, before realizing where I knew it from.

The tapestries. Only after we'd left this place behind did we realize they told the story of Weeks' journey to America, his intention to kidnap the children of Slattery Falls, luring them in, and finally even foretelling the collapse of the deadly house on the hill. I turned the tapestry over, searching for any sign of change, any hope that it would tell me what came next. A picture of the four of us leaving this place, for good this time. Maybe a picture of Weeks ensnared in some clever trap, never to reach from the beyond again.

But there was nothing. If this was fate, it did a shitty job of telling me what I was destined to do next.

Black soot covered every inch of the tapestry as though it had survived a fire, but only just. Fire, although I didn't remember there being any, had cleansed all of the prophetic shit from here.

Maybe what happened next was ours to tell.

Since the moment Weeks lectured us, Travis and I shared a sense of powerlessness that we rarely talked about, the unsettling feeling of not being in control of our own destiny.

With a smile creeping onto my face and tears ready to burst from my eyes, Robin's voice was a welcome relief. "Hey, guys, I've got our way out."

I dropped the tapestry to the floor like the piece of trash it was and turned toward her voice. Robin stood at the base of a staircase that had absolutely not been there five minutes ago. And for the first time in this fuck-faced basement's history, it didn't go down.

CHAPTER TWENTY-SEVEN

It wasn't easy to shake the feeling that we knew this landscape. You spend your whole life with everything in a fixed location. The streets that lead to work don't suddenly change places one day. When you open the door to your bedroom, you never find yourself in the kitchen. Shit just doesn't work that way, and it allows your brain to build schematics of the way everything is. The point is, it's very jarring when you emerge from a stairwell expecting to be in one place and you're not.

Needless to say, we didn't find ourselves at the top of the stone ramp overlooking the more tropical side of the grotto. A long hallway awaited us, and if not for the subtle lights floating along like a police spotlight seeking a criminal, I might not have known where we were. We'd opted against taking these stairs last time. I guess it turns out we could have gotten where we needed to go and avoided getting wet. Or not. Who fucking knows?

Travis started forward and I grabbed him, holding a finger over my lips.

"Listen," I whispered.

"Singing." Robin's voice trembled.

As soon as the tapping of our footsteps died away, I wondered how we ever missed it. Emily Stone wrote about the singing being too beautiful for the occasion, and that assessment was dead on. The music belonged in a church choir, although considering what kind of church would meet in a location like this sent chills up my spine.

I tiptoed forward, hoping we weren't about to see some Satanic ritual involving our daughter. I didn't check to see if Robin and Travis followed, but I heard their muffled footsteps. The scene was exactly how Emily described it, down to the finest detail. For all I knew, this house might have swept me back to the late 1800s, and did I really know that it hadn't?

Light danced across the walls, the focus more on blues and greens than I remembered, as if Weeks had gained control over even the color spectrum. The scene was so hypnotic that my eyes didn't immediately notice the dozen or so figures standing statue-still in that familiar shoulder-deep water.

Emily's description of the song didn't do justice to the real thing, but it hit the key points. An audience might describe a song as haunting, perfectly captured in the beauty of a minor key. It's almost like the only way the artist could harness the pain and intensity the music's final form demanded was to run it through a lens of sadness and ask it to become something transcendent.

That was this song. It made my skin crawl with its dissonant harmonies, traveling seamlessly between discord, each successive movement teasing resolution, but ultimately refusing to deliver on that promise. The melody made the hair stand up on the back of my neck, but as long as it continued, I could press on. I couldn't parse out a reason why, but I needed that music to continue once it entered my ears. It kept me feeling safe, although that made little sense.

I searched for any sign of April among the hooded figures. Although they were of various heights, none were slight enough to be a child. They must have taken her elsewhere.

But one of these fuckers would know where.

I stormed back to the stairway entrance, drawing strange looks from Robin and Travis. With a wave of my hand, I beckoned them to follow me. Once we found ourselves in close proximity, I whispered, hopeful the cavern's acoustics would allow the singing to drown out our voices.

"It's just like Emily's story. That means pretty soon here they'll start disappearing one by one."

"So what do you want to do?" asked Robin, in a tone that suggested she already knew the answer.

"If we barge in and disrupt the song, chances are there's a panic. Not to mention we're outnumbered. If we can time it right and grab the last one before they go under, maybe we can find out where April is."

"Won't they miss their final follower on the other side?" asked Travis.

"We're going to have to risk that. Feels like they're in some sort of trance, so who knows? Maybe not," I said, desperate to push my plan. "Robin, are you willing to shove a gun in their face if they get uncooperative?"

Robin sighed and pinched the bridge of her nose, a habit I seemed to bring out in her. "Does this suspect match the description of the person who allegedly murdered Bethany Stone, attacked you, then fled from her residence?"

Travis and I exchanged a quick smirk. Plausible deniability. I liked the cut of her jib.

"You bet," he said.

"Then I guess," said Robin, "I'd have no choice but to restrain him or her until the proper authorities arrive."

"Damn," I said, allowing a smile, "my phone doesn't get any service down here." The smile dropped. "You hear that?"

Travis and Robin both looked on in puzzlement.

"The song. It's getting softer. They must be starting to go under."

We crept back to the grotto opening. Sure enough, where twelve or more once stood, awaiting their journey into the next whatever, there were now only half that. Their song dwindled as their number did and we watched them sink below the surface, utterly positive they were making their way through the underground tunnel and to the other side.

As another descended, leaving only three more and a severely diminished choir, I tried to banish the notion of how little sense this place made, passing through the tunnel to reach the oversized dining room. These disciples of Weeks likely knew how to navigate this everchanging hellhole and could reach any destination of their choosing.

Three became two and we gestured in a silent attempt to assess which of the two would remain. While it's amazing how much you can read through eye contact when words aren't an option, I made a mental note to learn sign language if we got out of here alive.

The moment that number two's head disappeared beneath the water, we'd to rush the lone straggler. The bare-bones quality of the song would allow them to hear our advance, so we'd have to move quickly. Travis and I would do it, leaving Robin behind at the edge in case anything went awry.

Slowly, the figure on the left sunk beneath the surface, taking the harmony with it and leaving a male voice intoning the nonsense syllables like the world's slowest scat singer. The moment their head disappeared, we dove into the water and closed the ten-foot gap. I can't say whether the song continued because the next few seconds were all splashy chaos. Sneaking up and walking through the water might prove a little quieter but it sure as hell would have taken longer.

Travis and I crossed the grotto in seconds flat, arriving together. We seized the hooded figure around the arms and dragged him back to shore. He continued singing and even at this distance the hood provided enough shadow and the green glowing eyes enough distraction to make him unrecognizable.

Tossing him on the wet concrete of the shore didn't halt the song. This was definitely a trance.

"Where's April? Where's my daughter?" I shouted, grabbing his robes and yanking him to his feet. Song poured from beneath his hood, and I no longer found it alluring. I no longer cared what happened when the song came to an end. "You motherfucker!" I shook him harder, punctuating each syllable with a vicious thrashing.

I let him go and he hit the ground with a wet smack. The vocal performance pressed on but his body convulsed, shaking like a fish out of water. I looked at Robin and Travis as if to say *now what?* I didn't need them to open their mouths to tell me they had no idea. The gun came to mind, but I didn't suggest it. It would be no more effective than screaming my throat raw.

"Let me try," said Travis, ushering me aside. He straddled the prone body, still in the throes of some mad seizure. "Where are you going?" His tone demonstrated considerably more calm than mine and proved equally ineffective. He pointed to the grotto. "Where does that lead?"

More singing.

Travis looked up at me, a helpless expression on his face. He shrugged. "Fuck it."

He lifted his clenched right fist and drove it into the emerald-tinged darkness where a face would reside on any of God's normal creatures. The acoustics of the chamber and the sudden disappearance of the sweet tenor vocal line amplified the sickening crunch the man's nose made under Travis' fist. When he withdrew his hand, the green glow was gone.

Wide-eyed, Travis stared at the body.

"I love you, hon, but you're not strong enough to kill somebody with one punch. He's likely unconscious and you have a broken bone or two in your hand."

"I never punched anybody before," said Travis, shaking his hand and wincing, confirming at least one of those broken bones.

"Yep, no shit. Now, let's pull back that hood and see what we've got here."

Robin chuckled. "You make it sound like an episode of *Scooby Doo*."

"And we're the meddling kids. I'll take that," I said, pulling back the hood. If it was an episode of *Scooby Doo,* we undoubtedly would have recognized the man on the other side of the robe. Hell, Jeremiah Tedeschi or Chief Hempel would have sneered from beneath, waxing poetic about how they almost got away with it. But this man was as nondescript as they come. Short brown hair and eyes that shone gray, decidedly not green, hovered above a crooked, bloody nose and quivering lower lip. He was more catatonic than unconscious and his eyes exuded fear in batches. One look at Travis and Robin confirmed they didn't know this guy either.

"Where am I?" he asked, tears beginning to stream down his face. "And who are you people?"

CHAPTER TWENTY-EIGHT

A collective sigh rose from the three of us. Whoever this chump was, he either trained in theater or would prove as useless as nipples on a crocodile.

"As far as your questions go," said Robin, taking on the interrogator mantle, "all in good time. You seem confused and we'll help you as best we can, but there's a child missing, and we need to know what you're doing down here."

"Down where?" Fear gave way to frustration, and he got a little closer to yelling than I would have tolerated, but I deferred to Robin's expertise. "I don't know where this is or how I got here. Christ."

"Okay, a little give and take. I'm Officer Metcalf. What's the last thing you remember?"

If Robin's disclosure set the man at ease, he didn't show it. "Gil. Gil Baxter. I was at work. I run the bakery. Kneadful Things?"

Robin shook her head. Gil appeared disappointed. "I ducked into the backroom to get some flour and maybe rest my legs for a moment. A light flashed and next thing I know, I'm here, and why is my nose bleeding?"

Travis raised his hand. "I punched you because you wouldn't stop singing."

Gil frowned in a way I didn't realize facial muscles could pull off. Travis' response clearly provided more questions than answers.

"Was the light green?" I asked.

He narrowed his eyes, doing his best impersonation of a seventeenth-century puritan about to accuse me of witchcraft. "How could you know that?"

"It's kind of a theme," said Robin.

Gil nodded, clearly more willing to converse with an officer of the law than the sorceress and the bare-knuckle boxer. He opened his mouth to speak, then shut it, appearing to go green. As he raised a trembling finger to point behind us, it dawned on me Gil hadn't taken on a green pallor.

I spun around, expecting the lights from the grotto's bottom to have intensified, and nearly lost my footing when I saw the truth. Green light burst from beneath the water. I'd gotten used to not searching for the light source, as it remained ever elusive, and in order to not get stuck in one place or trapped in your own head down here, there were some things you had to shrug off and say "magic".

Not this one, however. Underneath the water, and approximately where I knew the tunnel to be located, a green circle sparked in a way that shouldn't have been possible. The water hummed, buzzing louder and louder, like a machine kicking into gear.

"That's it," I said.

Travis turned, looking at me like I had two heads. "What? What's it?"

"That's how we get to her."

He didn't answer. As if on cue, April's small voice drifted from the opposite side of the grotto. "Mommy."

Looking into Travis' eyes, I implored him to believe me, but his gaze held steel.

"It's a trick, Elsie. God dammit, can't you see that? It's too easy."

"We ignore this," I said, "and we get to spend the next hour or day or week lost in this fucking maze. Guess what, Travis? That's a fucking trick, too. So I'm going, and if you won't come with me, that's fine." I paused and took a deep breath. "I love you, Travis. I'll be with you no matter what, but I won't go home if I don't feel like we did everything in our power to get April back. And if he kills us? Fuck it, at least we'll all be together."

"You're crazy," he said, with a trace of a smile. He took my hand and squeezed it. "Let's go get our girl back."

I turned to the water and remembered Robin. "We've dragged you through a lot of shit, Robin. I understand if you want to wash your hands of us and escort Gil home."

Robin looked to Gil, still wallowing in fear on the cavern floor. "That's exactly what I should do." She shook her head. "But I won't forgive myself if I don't see this through. If something happens to you, Travis, or April that I could've stopped..." She murmured under her breath, "Oh, Robin, Penny is going to string you up." Looking to me, then Travis, then the glowing green circle of death, she said, "Fuck it. I'm all in."

I couldn't put into words what it meant to me, so I didn't try.

"Mr. Baxter?" asked Robin. "When you've got your wits about you, the staircase behind you should take you to the surface. I trust you can make your way home from there?"

He didn't answer, but scuttled toward the steps, vanishing into the darkness.

"That will take him home, right?" she asked.

"Stranger things have happened," I said, bunching up my shoulders.

"Um, Robin," said Travis. "What about the gun? Won't the water make it useless?"

"Waterproof," she said. "Supposed to be, anyway. I've never had to test it. The water will ruin the diary, though."

Shit.

She was right, but if its purpose was to get us here, then surely it wasn't necessary any longer. With no evident hiding places, I tucked it off to the side of the tunnel, hoping Gil wouldn't double back and grab a souvenir.

"I guess that's everything settled then." I waited for some other reason to delay, but it never came. I prepared to go first. It was always me first. Before we could change our minds, we dove one by one and disappeared into the brightly lit underwater tunnel.

CHAPTER TWENTY-NINE

Entering the tunnel, I recalled the dream from the previous night, my lungs nearly bursting in the never-ending pit of blackness under the water. Granted, it was due to being throttled by one of the green-eyed creatures, maybe even poor old possessed Gil back there, but truthfully I had no idea what came next. I'd swum through this tunnel four times while awake, but never when surrounded by green fire before.

Even underwater, my skin prickled as the murky water once more gave way to clear visibility, not unlike the kind you'd find in a swimming pool. We'd emerge from the other side and break the surface to find one of the surviving workers lying in wait for us. I was sure of it.

When we surfaced, the cavern was deserted. A momentary disappointment overtook me. The absence of a cult member trying to kill us actually made me sad. Go fucking figure. The walls gave no hints of what we might find, composed of drab gray stone and lending themselves nicely to the stagnant underground air. All focal points, real or imagined, led to the dry land where I usually found a staircase.

Travis rubbed his eyes. When he withdrew his hands, he blinked repeatedly.

"It's blurry," I whispered, my soft voice echoing throughout the chamber. "Isn't it? Like there's movement at the corner of your eyes, but when you turn your head, everything's normal."

"I've got that, too," said Robin.

Travis simply gawped.

"That's how it was the last time I came here alone," I said, allowing a little more volume into my voice.

"In your dream?" asked Travis.

I shook my head.

"It really happened," he amended. "God, Els, I'm so sorry. I didn't—"

"Me either. I wasn't completely sure, until… well, now."

Finding our feet, we climbed the slight incline to reach dry land. Where the flat portion of stone ended, a staircase led down. A gloomy darkness surrounded it, due more to the lighting of the cavern than anything physical lurking there. At least that was my hope.

Travis wrung water from his shirt. "Did you ever go down the staircase in your… last time?"

"Never," I said. "I always met the worker-thing right here. It gives me the same warning. It's a memory, not a premonition," I said, unsure of who I needed to convince.

Three will descend. Two will escape.

Oh shit. Had I put us right back in the same position? Brought Robin along only to have to sacrifice her? And how did April figure into that number? Questions raced through my mind faster than I could grab onto them, but so far, no prophetic figure. No prophecy, no death. Right?

Robin spoke, sending a jolt of surprise through me.

"Is that it?" whispered Robin. She aimed an accusatory finger at a shadow, hidden in the dimly lit area at the top of the stairs.

I opened my mouth to calm her nerves, but quickly closed it once more. It wasn't a shadow, but a figure hunched over, no higher than my chest. It shifted ever so slightly, almost flickering, but made no move to turn around. A black cloak covered its form, like the ones worn by both workers and possessed creatures. It didn't so much wear the robe as hide within it.

"April," I whispered, more hopeful than sure.

Travis stepped forward, an odd look on his face as he shook his head. He reached out as he crept forward, primed to yank the cloak from the figure. His hand trembled.

"Don't," I whispered, but without much force behind it.

He snatched the cloak and ripped it away.

Fear overtook me, but not the kind I'd felt down here before. A short burst of relief led the charge, doused quickly with disbelief. A blue hat with the orange NY logo. An illusion. It had to be. Brown hair curled out from underneath that hat, giving way to the rest of Josh's lanky frame, crouched down and facing away from us.

"Josh." Try as I might, I couldn't get my voice to rise above a whisper and he gave no acknowledgment that he'd heard me. Travis stepped back, the black cloak still dangling from his outstretched fingers. His mouth hung open just as loosely.

"Is that…?" Robin started, but either couldn't finish or decided her intrusion had not come at the best time.

With Travis frozen in place, I stepped forward cautiously. My light footsteps echoed but drew no reaction from Josh. An empty t-shirt sleeve sagged by his side. I pictured it so clearly, Weeks tearing Josh's arm off as effortlessly as shucking corn, then tossing it away like trash. Josh hadn't recovered his lost arm in death, or whatever this was. No blood stained the shirt or the ground surrounding him, leaving me even more confused. His left arm moved with a feverish intensity, as though he needed to finish building something before he could divert his attention.

My hand shook every bit as much as Travis'. I reached out and laid it on Josh's shoulder, immediately wishing I hadn't. His shirt offered only a thin layer of separation from his skin, which resembled porcelain. Never a fan of soaking up the sun, Josh had always displayed a pallor bordering on sickly, but a person couldn't achieve his newfound coloring if blood coursed through their veins. He almost seemed to glow.

I wish that were the worst part.

Dark spots dotted his face and arm, every inch of skin not covered by clothing and some that were. Stains was the first thought that came to mind. Decay was the second, and neither were dead on. They appeared like small voids, portions of Josh that ceased to exist. Small spots ranging from the size of a penny to that of a tennis ball spread across his body, inestimable without closer inspection, but north of twenty.

"What…?"

I looked into his eyes, thankfully free of the miniature abysses, and found recognition there before he looked away. His furiously busy left hand stopped and he turned, rising to his full height.

"Elsie," he said. His head craned to the side. "Travis, how did you get here?"

Travis and I looked at each other, still suspecting a trick, but unable to deny what lay before us. Travis spoke first. "We, uh, followed the, uh, green-eyed… things."

Josh nodded as though the explanation made perfect sense. "He waits."

"At the bottom of the stairs?" I asked, finishing the line from my first experience on this side of the grotto.

"Maybe." Josh's face and voice shared equal measures of puzzlement. "But I mean over here, on this side. I asked how you got here, but maybe that wasn't the right question. Do you know where you are?"

"The basement," said Travis, sounding anything but sure of his answer. "We came in a different way, but it has to be. Right?"

"You were. The house on your side has begun to reform, hasn't it? The underground portions, at least."

"Seems so."

"But you must have passed through the light to get here," said Josh.

"Green fire?" asked Travis, embarrassment lining the edge of his voice.

"It takes on different appearances, but yes, that sounds like it could be right. Travis, on your side…"

"Our side. *Our* side. You keep saying our side, but what the fuck does that mean? Josh…" Travis' voice faltered.

"If this place has a name, I don't know it. The afterlife? Another realm? Alternate dimension? It's all up for debate, although maybe now isn't the right time." Josh looked around expectantly. "Whatever it is, it's a place where things can happen that couldn't logically or scientifically take place on your side." He held his arm out as if to put himself on display. "Look at me. I'm dead on your side, buried under tons of rocks, yet you're speaking to me."

"How do we know it's really you? That you're not… some kind of trick." asked Travis.

Josh shrugged, rocking back and forth on his heels. "You're welcome to ask me anything you like to confirm your suspicions."

I looked at Travis. "I don't know. The way he talks kind of does it for me."

Travis didn't answer. "What's the safe word?"

A smile formed on Josh's lips just to the side of a quarter-sized black hole. "It's hardly time for that yet. You just got here."

Travis clenched his fists and squinted his eyes. He looked at me. "He doesn't know. It's a fucking trick."

"If it were," said Josh. "You'd have every right to be upset, making that sentence a perfect place to use the word 'fuck' for emphasis."

At that, I rushed forward and hugged Josh. He wrapped his arm around me, but didn't squeeze. Something still felt off.

"I *am* dead," he said, as if reading my thoughts. "I must be. I remember it all. The pain…" He glanced at his empty sleeve. "When Weeks hit me, it only hurt for a moment."

"I'm so sorry, Joshie," I whispered.

With glistening eyes, Travis stepped in and hugged him as well.

After a moment, Robin cleared her throat. Travis and I stepped back.

I wiped my eyes. "Oh, uh, Josh. This is Robin Metcalf. She's been helping us with some stuff on the other side."

"April?" he asked, and my heart nearly burst from my chest.

"Is she here?" Robin whispered.

"I've seen her a few times. It's why I'm up here, actually."

I furrowed my brows and motioned for him to go on.

"I've been waiting for you two. I hoped you might find your way here eventually." His eyes bounced back and forth between Travis and me, always staring at something just over our shoulders. "See, this is all on me."

"What does that mean?" asked Travis.

"Long story short? Weeks has been drawing his power from this place for centuries, but he never could figure out how to get here. He managed to send others, but couldn't seem to push across the boundary himself. I can't be sure, but I think he suspects that if he could get here and return to your world, the immortality, the power? That would be nothing compared to what he would be able to achieve next." Josh hesitated. "Long story short is I made a mistake. A bad one."

Josh trained his eyes on the ground. "As it turns out, it's much easier to bring something over from this world to yours than vice versa."

"Or someone," said Travis.

"Tabitha," I added. My stomach performed an impromptu gymnastics routine.

"She brought him here," said Josh. "And it was exactly what he wanted."

"Wouldn't that make this a form of afterlife, though?" I asked.

Josh shook his head. "There's a… I don't know, like a residue, almost when someone has ties to both worlds. It's what happened to me. I'm the summoner. Part of me got pulled along for the ride. This is home now, or as close to it as I'm liable to get." He studied one of the voids lining his arm like track marks on a junkie. "If you think this is bad, you should see Tabitha. And it's all my fault."

"What are those?" asked Travis, now that it didn't feel impolite to point them out.

"Nothing," he said, lowering his arm.

"Jesus, Josh. They're obviously not—"

"No, no. They're nothing. Little pieces of non-existence. Every time Weeks borrows from me or Tabitha, he makes us use that residue to connect the worlds, a small piece of us is lost to… Honestly, I don't know where." A pause, then he whispered, "It's like a penance paid to this place."

Silence took over the cavern.

"Chin up, Elsie. It just may happen that oblivion is better than here."

"Well, can't you come back over to our side? You can connect the worlds, travel between them. You said it yourself!"

A small grin lit his face but didn't touch his eyes. "It doesn't work that way. Besides, this is supposed to be the short version, remember?"

I nodded, unsure of what to say next. Suddenly, visions of April returned to my head, like a blaring alarm clock.

"April," I nearly shouted. "She's okay, right?"

Josh looked down and behind him.

"I can damn well tell when you're lying," I said. "Don't you dare!"

"No, she's safe. She is." He kept his eyes on the floor. "This is just guesswork, Elsie, but I believe Weeks thought it would be the ultimate revenge to feed her to this place, like he fed all the others. He has her here, but she's safe. I made sure of that."

"How sure are you?" I asked.

"I'm not privy to everything that happens here, and I avoid contact with him when I can, but it only makes sense. We know he's a creature of vengeance, and he needs her to get what he wants from me."

"What did you do?" asked Travis, fear overriding the suspicion in his tone.

"I made a deal." Josh stepped aside to reveal what he'd been working on when we entered—a pile of straw dolls, each one individually crafted and lashed together with red twine.

"I take it you've seen these before?"

"Seen them. Read about them. What the hell are they?" I asked.

"Talismans," he said. Emily Stone's word. "They began as a way for him to try and cross over here, hundreds of years ago. Weeks imbued each one with power from this place and had them hidden strategically throughout town. But that never worked. It was never going to. Now that he can draw directly from the source, it might. Especially with the people who can walk between worlds creating them. Adding... potency."

"He's been holding April hostage to get you to make these?" Fire and fury pervaded my question.

"It's complicated, but yes," said Josh. "A byproduct of the process is he doesn't even have to be near people to possess them anymore. If someone wanders too close to one of these things, he can reach out and grab them." He looked at the still-fresh bruises on my neck. "Is that what happened to you?"

I lifted my hands to cover my neck. "What's the endgame?"

"Well, with enough of these things spread throughout town, he could theoretically open that hole you fell in large enough to come through it."

"Fucking hell," said Travis. "How big is he now?"

"Size doesn't matter, Travis. It's power. Ability. Also, kudos for not giggling at my choice of words." Josh grinned. "You three came through no problem because, apologies, you have limited power, same as the others."

"The hoods," said Travis.

"Exactly. You're like, um, bugs."

"Thanks, Josh." I paused. "So what happens next?"

His grin dropped. "You go get her. I have to wait here, but I'll be ready to send you back."

"Can't you—?"

He shook his head.

"But won't sending us back cause more of…?" I gestured all along his body.

He stared at the black holes and shrugged once more. "Absolutely. But as I said, sometimes the unknown is better."

CHAPTER THIRTY

It was a lot to take in. My cousin was fading away to oblivion, my daughter remained in the clutches of some ancient ghost, demon, or maybe just an asshole with too much power, and here we were descending more fucking stairs to try and snatch her back.

He waits. The voice echoed through my head. Not real this time, but a memory.

I came to a skidding stop on the step. Travis nearly plowed me over.

"What is it?" he said, swiveling his head like a deer on the lookout for a wolf.

"He knows we're here," I said.

Robin's face blanched, visible even in the dim stairwell light.

"He always knows," said Travis, with a shrug. "We never let that stop us before."

I shook my head, then continued down the stairs at a slower clip, mostly because I didn't want to look at his face when I said what was on my mind. "It didn't matter before. It was just us. We were stupid kids risking our asses. Now there's April to consider. What if he hurts her? What would we do?"

"He won't."

I laughed. I couldn't help it. "That's fucking naive and you know it. How many kids has he sacrificed to this other side? And he's gonna spare ours because he made Josh a pinky promise?"

"Elsie," Robin interrupted, her Officer Metcalf authority showing its plumage.

I froze again and turned to her.

"I won't pretend I fully understand any of this, but I've worked more missing children's cases than I care to count. Positivity won't dictate the outcome, but neither will negativity. What negativity will do is clog the gears and slow everything down, decreasing the chances of finding the child."

I wanted to hit her. Instead, I shot her a venomous look. Whether the lighting allowed it to shine through for full effect, I don't know, but she didn't change her firm stance. A stand-off, if ever there was one. I backed down first because somewhere in my convoluted mind, I knew she was right. Even now, our staring contest pissed the time away while I tried to prove my attitude wasn't detrimental.

"You should apologize," whispered Travis. The acoustics made sure our secret didn't stay between us, but the sly grin on his face gave away the joke. It lightened the atmosphere enough to let us move forward as something resembling a united front.

The stairs did not lead us into the dining hall because we were in another realm or something. I still didn't entirely understand that aspect. Instead, they emptied us into an unfamiliar room, although room wasn't the right word. It possessed the same cave-like quality of the cavern, with rough-hewn walls and a dank stagnant odor permeating the air, but the decor seemed borrowed from Weeks' original house. No larger than an average living room, this cave came furnished with several wooden chairs lined with red velvet, a matching sofa, and a footstool. The cozy layout spoke of meticulous planning. Put up some tacky wallpaper and an antique lamp and it could have passed for grandmother's house.

"This place never fucking ceases to surprise me," I said.

Travis opened his mouth to speak, but a series of *clicks* interrupted him.

Two lamps beamed on, materializing on end tables next to the chairs, and I swear they didn't exist before those clicking sounds. Even the tables that held the lamps hadn't stood there a moment before.

"Mommy."

The voice was so tiny and so quiet. I suspected it came from far away, perfectly situated to lead me toward another heaping helping of running through rock mazes and other supremely unhelpful shit.

"Baby," said Travis, his voice quivering. At first I thought he spoke to me. My heart broke in two imagining what could affect him like that.

Then I turned, and there she was.

Like the tables and lamps, April hadn't been in the room a moment ago, but now sat in one of the fuzzy chairs, rubbing her hands up and down the armrest. The friction created a whooshing sound that echoed through the cave. Before I could process what I saw, Travis was on her. He whisked her out of the seat and into the air. I half expected April to vanish at his touch, and I think that would have destroyed me. Instead, she remained in his grip as he planted kisses on each small cheek, drowning her in mumbled adulations.

Only she didn't look happy.

Sensing something wrong, Travis lowered April to the ground. I wrapped her in a too-tight hug, needing to feel her with my own hands to confirm this wasn't another fucking illusion.

"He waits." That same tiny voice, only more flat this time.

I released April from the hug and leaned back, staring into her bright green eyes.

"They used to be blue," boomed an all-too-familiar voice. "Or had you forgotten already?"

I stood, shepherding April behind me. Travis stepped in front of me. Robin drew her gun and aimed it at the roiling darkness in the far corner of the room, the portion that spoke.

More lights flickered on, the source unidentifiable. Additional lamps? Fucking lightning bugs? Who knew? Expecting an eight-foot-tall monster, I was taken aback to see an almost human-looking version of Robert Weeks. Nonetheless, the being who'd played boogeyman for the past decade and a half stood before us. Strands of gray intermingled with his flaming red hair and beard, and while his sea-green eyes didn't glow, they possessed a gentle calm more chilling than anger.

"Don't even think about touching the girl," Robin roared. Her eyes narrowed and her teeth clashed together as she leveled the gun at Weeks' head.

"Or what?"

The gun flew from Robin's hand before she could respond. Weeks effortlessly caught it and displayed it in one massive palm. His face remained impassive as the gun turned to dust and blew away on a nonexistent breeze.

Robin's battle face gave way to saucer-sized eyes and a gaping mouth. She took a step backward and I don't believe she even knew it.

Weeks shook the remaining debris off his hand, then gestured to the sofa. "Please, sit."

"Not on your fucking life," growled Travis, cementing himself between April and Weeks.

"Suit yourself." He took a step back and sat in a recliner resting in the previously darkened portion of the room. One of a pair. As soon as the light revealed the second chair, I almost screamed, but it caught in my throat.

"Tabitha," I whispered.

"Jesus fucking Christ," said Travis.

The last time we'd seen Tabitha, her spirit appeared draped in white from head to toe. She had a harsh look about her that the ethereal glow transformed into beauty. What became of her, I didn't have to guess. Josh had told us. Whereas the voids appeared almost like an outbreak of measles on him, they devoured Tabitha's features. Her misshapen body caved into itself, as if succumbing to the black holes. One such void took up her entire forehead, enveloping one of her eyes and pulling the other out of line giving her the look of a cyclops from Greek mythology. Another resided on her lower cheek, pulling her mouth into a gnarled rictus of agony. Her constantly moving fingers, likely searching for the materials to craft more dolls, were the only thing that gave any sign of life. Weeks had transformed his once-bride into a wretched creature.

I gritted my teeth. "What did you do to her?"

Weeks turned to regard Tabitha, furrowing his brows as if he'd forgotten she was there. "Only what was necessary," he said, turning back. Despite his appearance, Weeks wasn't human and maybe never had been.

"You got her back and you still craved more. You fucking monster!"

"When you live as long as I have, you understand that people are rarely who you think they are. Tabitha cared far more about controlling me than helping me to be the best man I could be. In the end, I will suffer through her sacrifice."

"And April? Was that necessary?" From the corner of my eye, I saw Robin take a step back toward the stairwell, her arms covering April. Was it my imagination or had the green in April's eyes rescinded a little?

Weeks caught me looking. "Once back in your world, the spell will wear off. Her eyes will return to their putrid shade of baby blue. I've done her a kindness, you know."

"A kindness?" said Travis, not bothering to disguise the disgust in his voice.

"Of course. She won't remember her time here. She's free to go, now that I have you."

I didn't think about the consequences, simply trusted gut instinct. The clashes and mistrust between Robin and me disappeared in a heartbeat. "Robin, take her! Go now!"

If she shot a questioning look, it was fleeting and I missed it. I heard feet pounding up the steps and they were gone. Josh would ferry them back to the other side. I didn't understand how it worked, but he made sacrifices even in death to keep his niece safe.

Weeks made no move to stop them. He didn't even flinch.

"Why us?"

"Actually, dear, it's just you I need. Travis is quite free to go."

Travis narrowed his eyes but didn't say a word. He reached out and took my hand. He squeezed it so tight, the metal of his wedding band bit into my finger. A comforting pain. In the corner, Tabitha made a strange wheezing noise that made my skin crawl. A warning?

I did my best to ignore it. "Fine then, why me?"

Weeks sat forward, hands on his thighs. "If I'm to be entirely honest,

I wasn't sure why until recently. Something drew me to the three of you initially. It's like they say, when your body craves a certain food, red meat for instance, it may be that it needs iron to function. I didn't know why I needed to collect you, but I did."

"Get to the fucking point," said Travis.

Weeks smirked. "Very well. Let's cut to the chase, shall we? You are able to cross between worlds, Elsie. Think back. You've done it before today, haven't you?"

The dream resonated in my head, a memory of my first trip here, illuminated in green light.

His smirk pulled back toward his ears. "Yes, that's what I thought. And you didn't need an ancient spell to enable that power, did you?"

He didn't need my answer to that. Weeks rose to his feet. "Tell me, what were your first impressions when I appeared before you tonight?"

Travis and I inched back toward the staircase, keeping silent.

A frantic buzzing blared from above, resembling a surge of electricity, disappearing almost as quickly as it began. The noise froze us in our tracks. Travis gazed toward the jagged, cave-like ceiling, but I fixed my attention on Weeks. Arrogance bled from his face and his smile dropped at the onset of the sound, a momentary glimpse of mortality. Of something almost anxious.

What was up there that could drain the hubris from the man who dwelt in our nightmares?

He recovered quickly and continued, "I appear almost human. This is my form here, in my home, my prison. Tabitha, before her unfortunate incident, did not glow with a white-hot heat here. She simply existed." His eyes became vacant for a moment then regained a cunning gleam. "Once back on the other side, my form will be… Well, I really can't think of a better word than limitless. You, Elsie, will help me open a gateway to Slattery Falls and allow me back through."

"Fuck you."

The room shook as he stepped forward. Even when the rumbling ceased, my knees continued to wobble. "My dear, you don't have a choice."

CHAPTER THIRTY-ONE

I knew this moment, remembered it from last time. The room quakes with a ferocity that puts the last tremor to shame. The lights cast from the lamps flash red, or maybe green this time, and Weeks grows exponentially, towering and ready to stomp us out like vermin.

Only none of that happened. Weeks returned to his chair, tenting his fingers on his lap.

Travis yanked me toward the staircase, ready to join Robin and April. Weeks couldn't follow us back to our world. Not directly. A violent wind whooshed by and pulled Travis off his feet. I spun to see him floating in the air, anchored only by his grip on my hand.

"No!" I screamed, and the wind jerked harder. It avoided me, focusing all its energy on Travis. I squeezed his hand with everything I had, but felt his fingers slipping away. With my heels dug in and teeth gritted, I pulled as hard as I could, but the wind blasted through with a final vicious burst. Travis' fingertips brushed mine as he flew up the staircase, smacking into the wall with a sickening crack.

I lunged forward to follow, but the doorway shrunk in a swirling pattern as he disappeared into the rapidly diminishing darkness. With my arm still outstretched, frantically reaching for Travis' grip, the wall transformed to solid concrete. Weeks stole something I loved every time he intruded on my life.

"I won't chase you this time," he said, looking down at his hands.

"Where is he?" I demanded, storming across the room.

"On his way home, I would expect. Or perhaps whiling away eternity with my new gatekeeper. It is no concern of mine, nor yours."

My heart sank as his last statement clicked some cogs into place. Was this the way out? If Weeks could be trusted, and that was a substantial *IF,* then April was safe and Travis had the opportunity to join her. Hardheaded as Travis might be, surely Josh would talk some sense into him. Weeks had granted him a stay of execution and sticking around would burn that down to the wick fast.

The room, previously a half-furnished cave, evolved before my eyes.

The jagged walls smoothed into a solid color that more closely resembled drywall than stone, but still lacked doors and windows. All of the sudden, the furniture no longer appeared out of place, but presented an almost inviting aura.

I collapsed onto the couch. Weeks lifted his head and fixed a curious gaze on me.

"No fighting? No more yelling and cursing? Am I to understand you're giving up that easily?"

"Not giving up," I said. I clucked my tongue before turning his own words against him. "Only doing what's necessary."

"To save them."

I nodded, lost in thought.

"I can appreciate that." Something resonated in his voice almost like empathy and that was too much. I trained my eyes on his and hoped he saw the fire that burned behind them.

"How could you ever fucking understand that?" He didn't answer and that was fine because I wasn't done. "You've never given a shit about anyone enough to save them. You know, one thing we never considered, not even Josh, was with all the power-sucking from this plane of existence, how come you never brought Tabitha back yourself?"

His face reddened, matching the hue of his beard. "I tried."

"Oh, the fuck you did! It took Josh a couple days on the internet to learn how to summon her. You're telling me you couldn't figure it out after centuries, if not fucking eons, to dig into every dark and restricted Necronomicon-esque book in existence?"

Robert Weeks' green eyes blazed. Veins corded on his neck, telling of his struggle to resist flying across the room to tear me in half. Fuck it, I was already as good as dead. The room had no exits. I'd stopped searching a few minutes ago. Just me and Weeks, not to mention the shell of Tabitha, occupying her corner in a near-vegetative state. Unintelligible grunts replaced that soft wheeze emanating from her. A faint hue of green surrounded her, the only inkling of anything supernatural in the room. Weeks turned his chair away from her ever so slightly.

"If you are trying to goad me into killing you, it won't work," said Weeks. His tone suggested it might work after all.

I shrugged. "I'm not trying to do anything, but I won't sit here and let you put yourself in the same boat as me. You wouldn't so much as pull a chair out for Tabitha, and don't try to argue the point. She's disappearing into nothingness for your chance to what? Come back to Earth One and rule as some sort of overlord?"

He remained silent, refusing to turn and look at Tabitha no matter how many times I gestured in her direction.

I sat forward on the couch. "You are a coward." I'd meant to put more venom behind it, but a strange thing happened on the short journey from brain to tongue. I realized it wasn't an insult, but a fact. It came out devoid of emotion and with the hint of a question mark attached to it.

He answered, but only after taking two deep breaths. "You are entitled to your opinion. I would disagree. However, one thing you should consider is who will dictate the amount of comfort you will be in during your time here."

"My time here?"

Invisible insects crawled across my skin as a grin settled back in on his face. "You've seen Josh. Seen *her*." Despite the refusal to use her name, he gestured to Tabitha, who seemed to glow even brighter than before. "You won't last long. The energy required to aid me in transcending worlds? I believe it's in you, but with no reserves."

"So you're going to force me to do some arts and crafts projects, whittle up some straw dolls, and then you're going to plug me in until the juice runs out?"

"You don't sound as if the notion frightens you."

"Does it work better if I'm scared?"

"I suppose it matters not." The way he studied me, his eyes crawling with curiosity, made me suspect he was holding something back.

In the corner, Tabitha's grunting increased in both frequency and volume. Weeks' head twitched, but he kept his gaze on me.

"And what if I won't do it?" I whispered.

"You will." The arrogance in his voice made my blood boil. "You've seen my ability to send others to your world to complete my work."

"And kill me?"

He waved his hand. "That was a mistake. You were not supposed to be there. Time can be… strange, unpredictable, in the journeys back and forth. That diary was supposed to be removed before you ever stumbled across it."

"We wouldn't have found our way here without the diary."

A knowing grin crossed his face. "That's not true and you know it. You would have camped out in the rubble if that's what it took to get the little brat back. Besides, I put everything you needed to know in the dreams."

"You?"

I let the thread hang, suspecting he'd be happy to dance in circles around the truth for as long as necessary. Rather than answer, he inspected his nails with a bored look on his face, then cleared his throat.

"To your original point, it's no accident that I've sent Travis and April home. I will keep tabs on them. Should you refuse to comply, I can have them brought back in a snap, or dealt with on the other side."

My eyes widened as I shot up straight. Weeks chuckled, but it wasn't his threat that drew my expression. A hand had emerged from the void in Tabitha's chest, now ringed with green fire. The hand's fourth finger wore a familiar black wedding band.

The flaming circle grew wider little by little and the hand reached out, beckoning with its pointer finger. I crossed my arms and stood, actively avoiding any glances at Tabitha. I began to pace, hoping to convince Weeks it was only nervous energy.

"And what if I decided I was done? Tried to escape?" I moved to the side of the couch, far enough from Tabitha that her newfound portal wouldn't draw his eye, but setting myself up for a straight sprint. Twenty years spanned between junior year track and late-thirties Elsie, but I don't remember the stakes being quite so high back then.

"You couldn't. There are no exits if I wish there not to be." He began to survey the room as if unsure.

"Hypothetically," I blurted out in an attempt to regain his attention. I kicked at the firm ground in what I hoped was a gesture of nonchalance, surprised to find it had sprouted carpet at some point.

He replied with that same grin. It had become disturbingly familiar and reinforced every ideal I held about his character. Despite appearances, the man left his humanity behind ages ago. His body eschewed his soul and all that remained was a husk where his heart used to beat—a cavern full of hate and insecurity.

"I will always find you."

My leg muscles tensed, coiled springs ready to unleash their stored energy. "Yep," I said, anticipating that very answer. "That sounds like a problem for another day."

He scrunched his brow and sat forward. I launched toward Tabitha, desperately trying to outrun a snap of his fingers, and dove through the expanding hole in her chest. Green light surrounded me for the space of a second, and then it was gone.

"Go, go, go. No time. No time," a voice shouted as the tropical half of the grotto materialized around me. Josh waved toward the water, a grimace of pain stamped across his features. It hadn't been an hour since our first encounter, yet his face erupted with those voids, some quite larger than before—evidence of my miraculous escape.

Travis grabbed my arm before I could get my bearings and ushered me into the crystal-clear pool, which blazed with green light.

A roar blasted up the staircase behind Josh, no doubt opened once more at the bottom. Footsteps boomed from below. More than just one pair.

"Come with us!" I shouted. He shook his head, a sad smile on his face.

"It still doesn't work like that." He paused as the footsteps grew louder. Closer. More frantic.

"I love you too, Joshie."

"Husky," he whispered.

Green light enveloped Travis and me as we dashed into the water. Weeks exploded from the top of the stairs, arms outstretched, but too late. He didn't say a word. He didn't need to. His eyes said it all.

I will always find you.

CHAPTER THIRTY-TWO

The glaring sea-green of Weeks' eyes burned in my retinas as we surfaced on the other side, emerging from the rapidly fading portal submerged in the now-murky water. I shut my eyes before I could get my bearings, afraid we'd still be back in that other dimension, whatever the fuck it was. Josh had tried to explain it, Weeks too, but either my high school diploma was past its expiration date or the weird shit surrounding this place had grown odd to an illogical degree.

Eyes still blocking out the world, I clutched Travis tight, listening to his heavy breathing begin to calm—a signal that maybe our pursuers were gone. Unfortunately, that meant Josh, or what was left of him, was gone with them. I wanted to keep the world at bay for a little longer. Then I remembered April and swam across the grotto, Travis close behind.

The hallway that usually waited at the edge of the water was gone, replaced by a single stair set with a dim green glow at the top. The choice became a lot easier when the house removed alternative options. My heart sank as I stared at the base of the stairs. Emily Stone's diary was gone, stolen by someone or swallowed by this place. A glimmer of hope flashed. Perhaps Robin had scooped it up on her way out. I clutched at that shred of optimism, unwilling to let its ember die.

Still dripping, Travis sidled up to me and took my hand. "Ready?"

I exhaled slowly. "Ready." We ascended the stairs to greet the fresh air and hug our little girl.

As we stepped from the doorway, the woods surrounded us. A warm breeze rustled the leaves on the trees, barely covering the soft hum from the still-glowing stone entry. Something about the sound unsettled me, but my nerves were shot, so I brushed it off for the time being. Each darkened gap between tree trunks threatened the return of a hooded figure, causing us to proceed with our heads on a swivel.

The moon's light breached the canopy with more success than earlier, despite the fact that trees appeared more full. It hadn't been a faulty treeline bathing us in dark any more than defective iPhone flashlight apps. I pulled my phone from my pocket, thankful the screen hadn't shattered from recklessly tossing my body around. I'd be sore tomorrow, but as long as I could hold April while I iced my old ass, I didn't care. Surprisingly, the flashlight performed its duties admirably, igniting the night air and showing us the way back to the ruined grounds. My heart sank a little when I didn't see April and Robin.

No worries, I told myself. *They got themselves to safety. Can't keep a five-year-old in the woods all night.*

"She'd freeze," I said.

"Hm?" said Travis, as we acknowledged each other for the first time since coming above ground.

"Just thinking out loud."

"It's not that cold, actually," he added, absently.

I pulled him close and wrapped my arms around him. "You came back for me."

A goofy grin lit up his face and he kissed me. "I'm sorry, was there another option?"

"It's not that I didn't think you would. I just didn't know if you could."

His face took on a serious demeanor. "Well, I hate to think what's happening to Josh right now. This is twice now he's taken a pickaxe to Weeks' plans."

My stomach dropped at the thought of Josh. "I was ready to give up, you know. If it meant you and April could be safe."

"You're not... mad, are you?" he asked, the most genuine look of confusion I'd ever seen spread across his face.

"No. No, of course not," I said, forcing a smile. "It's just, Weeks is going to come back. I think it might have been over if I'd stayed there."

"What the fuck, Elsie?" His voice stayed level and calm, but I didn't miss the tinge of anger present.

"Hey," I said, grabbing his face and pulling it toward mine. "When I saw your hand coming through, I didn't have to go with you. God, I didn't *want* to stay. I just... Shit, Travis, I thought this was over until a few days ago. Now the world is upside down again. You know?"

Travis' edge subsided as he pressed a light kiss against my cheek, then took my hand and started walking again. "Yeah. Yeah, I get that. I'd made my peace with losing Josh. Felt like things were going right, so of course that obnoxious fuck would set up a game of mousetrap to lure you in." He paused. "You're right. It's not over."

"Not by a long shot. Total speculation, but I think he'll need time to regroup. Maybe days, maybe years. We've got time to get ready, but we have to assume it's not much."

He looked up at the moon and raised an eyebrow.

"What?" I asked.

"Nothing," he said, keeping his eyes locked on the night sky. "Start tomorrow?"

A laugh shot out that I couldn't have managed only a few minutes before.

"You have Robin's number still?"

Keeping the flashlight trained in front of us, I scrolled through my calls and found it, then pressed Send. "Shit, no service."

He pulled his phone from his pocket. "Yeah, me either."

Our luck didn't change as we emerged into the clearing. A swift glance in every direction brought no sightings of green-eyed lackies. It seemed that all Robert Weeks' deviants were either out of commission or very competent spies.

The idea of this ruined foundation with all of Weeks' belongings festering away, yet left almost as a monument, a graveyard, seemed strange. We assumed the town abandoned it to try and erase the history, but we didn't know that for certain. Perhaps, just like in the distant past, they tried to burn it all, and the house, or what was left of it, simply said "no".

"Oh motherfucker," said Travis, snapping me away from my thoughts. I didn't need to ask what the outburst was about.

Travis threw his hands up. "Did, uh, did we get towed?"

We walked in circles around where we knew we had left the car, but against all odds, neither ours nor Robin's vehicles appeared out of thin air.

"I really fucking hate this," I said. "Why would she have moved our car? How even?"

Travis shook his head, no attempt at an explanation.

Another glance at my phone and still no bars. "Shall we walk to town?"

Travis held the crook of his elbow out to me. I took it and off we went, trying to make mental heads or tails out of yet another fucked-up situation.

We had barely reached the base of the hill before the first pair of headlights caught us. Travis jumped into the middle of the road to flag down the red sedan. I didn't recognize the model. The driver skidded to a stop on the side of the road and climbed out with a welcoming smile plastered across his face. Friendly or not, he kept the open door between us and him.

"You folks need a lift?" the man asked. He was tall, thin, and spoke with a stereotypical north shore accent. At least we were home.

"Oh man, thank you," said Travis. "That would be great."

"My pleasure, sir. Where you headed?" he asked, dropping every R.

Travis looked to me. "Maybe into town," I said. "Actually, would you mind if I used your phone real quick? If it has service, that is."

The smile dropped and a look of confusion took hold. I waited for a green flash in each eye to complete the transformation, but the eyes, though narrowed, remained blue.

Just like April's.

"Yeah, sure," he said, digging it from his pocket and unlocking it with some sort of retinal scan.

I snatched the phone in a very Gollum-like manner, probably making the poor bastard regret pulling over. My hand shook so much it took a few tries to type Robin's number into the phone before pressing Send.

Ring.

Ring.

Ring.

Come on, dammit. Where the hell had this woman gone with our daughter?

"Hello?" A young woman answered. Whoever she was, her annoyed tone told me I'd dragged her from sleep.

"Um, uh, yeah. Hello. I'm looking for, uh, Robin. Officer Metcalf."

The girl took so long to chime back in I thought the call had dropped. I pulled it away from my head to check, but it had full service.

"Who's calling?"

I tried to keep the irritation from my voice, but this woman stood between me and April. "Tell her it's Elsie. We just want to know where she went."

A pause and a sniffle. "That's not funny." The line went dead.

Staring in frustrated disbelief at the phone, I snuck a glance at Travis and the driver engaged in conversation. I took a few deep breaths and sent the same number through, ready to shout the girl down when she picked up again.

"Hello?" Robin this time—I was almost sure of it—although her voice sounded slightly more gruff over the phone, as if she'd come down with a cold.

"Robin, is that you—"

"I don't know who this is, but you've upset my daughter terribly. Don't call here again!"

"Wait, wait, wait!" I screamed. The conversation between Travis and the driver halted in its tracks. Slowly, they stared over at me. "Robin, don't hang up. It's me, it's Elsie." The line went quiet again and I was sure she'd ended the call, then her voice came back, softer than before.

"Elsie. Is it really you?"

"Yes, we're just outside of town. Where are you? Where's April?"

"You don't sound any different at all."

"Robin! You're scaring me. Where did you take her?"

Another silence, although this time I could hear her breathing. Finally, "You just spoke to her."

Travis eased toward me, a look of concern etched upon his face. The driver stayed by the car, equally nervous, but for altogether different reasons.

My heart pounded in my chest and suddenly there wasn't enough air. "What do you mean?" I asked, just above a whisper.

"Elsie, it's been eleven years since April and I left you in Slattery Falls."

The story concludes in:

THE WORLD YOU LOVED

Slattery Falls, Book Three

ACKNOWLEDGMENTS

What a journey this book has gone through. *Slattery Falls* was originally meant to be a standalone book, but I've always had trouble leaving ambiguity out of my endings. Needless to say, the door was always open a crack. Ken McKinley of Silver Shamrock believed in this story enough to encourage me to write a second and third entry. Unfortunately, Silver Shamrock closed its doors after this book was finished, but before it could enter the world.

A massive thank you to David Niall Wilson and David Dodd at Crossroad Press for rereleasing *Slattery* and giving *Decimated Dreams* and the third installment a home. It wasn't until I sat down to write that I realized these characters still had a lot to say, and how much I'd missed them.

Once again, Donnie Goodman killed it on the cover design, finding a perfect way to blend my inane ideas with classic horror and somehow tie it together with the first book. It's been a genuine pleasure, man.

Erica Robyn and Tyler Jones offered incredibly insightful beta notes on the entire book and shaped it from a story with potential to a story I could be proud of. I am endlessly thankful to the two of you for your help, support, and the fact that you don't get sick of my constant botherations.

Patrick McDonough answered every late-night text and phone call searching for affirmation that I was going in the right direction and not just continuing a story that had run its course. His friendship and encouragement have proved invaluable to this thing I call a writing career.

To Aron, at its heart this is a book about the trials and tribulations of a marriage on its rockiest shores. Two people being there for each other through thick and thin. I couldn't have written it without having experienced that by your side. The line from the dedication comes from our wedding song, "Pistol" by Dustin Kensrue. To this day, I can't hear that song without imagining the smile on your face during our first dance.

Speaking of music, it's a trifle odd to thank someone(s) who will likely never read it, but the title of the book comes from the My Chemical Romance song, "Welcome to the Black Parade". Every time I hit a wall, all it took was a trip through MCR's 2006 album, *The Black Parade*—namely the aforementioned song, "Sleep", and "Famous Last Words"—and my gears would start to turn again. This book wouldn't have turned out quite the same without that musical masterpiece.

Thanks to Ross Jeffery, Anthony J. Rapino, Heather Levy, and Patrick R. McDonough for early reads and kind words. There was never a scarier time than waiting to hear back about whether this book needed to exist, and your praise of this middle portion of the story made it all worthwhile.

A final thank you to some people in horror whose support make it possible to sit down and write every day: Ronald Kelly, John Lynch, Chance Forshee, William Sterling, Hailey Piper, Christa Carmen, Briana Morgan, Cina Pelayo, Janine Pipe, Steve Stred, RJ Joseph, Andrew Robert, Michael Clark, Vivian Kasley, Jeremy Hepler, Candace Nola, Brian Bowyer, Lee Murray, and Kevin Whitten among many others.

And you, dear reader, thanks for sticking around. Stay tuned for *The World You Loved: Slattery Falls, Book Three.*

About the Author

Brennan LaFaro is a horror writer living in southeastern Massachusetts with his wife, two sons, and his hounds. An avid lifelong reader, Brennan also co-hosts the Dead Headspace podcast. *Slattery Falls*, the first entry in a trilogy, is out now from Crossroad Press. Be on the lookout for *Noose*, coming soon from Dark Lit Press. You can read his short fiction in various anthologies and find him on Twitter at @brennanlafaro or at www.brennanlafaro.com.

CROSSROAD
PRESS

Made in United States
North Haven, CT
14 December 2022

28674804R00086